THE VIXEN'S SCREAM

A captivating murder mystery featuring DCI Jack Harris

JOHN DEAN

THE BOOK FOLKS

Paperback published by The Book Folks

London, 2017

ISBN 978-1-5213-9197-6

www.thebookfolks.com

THE VIXEN'S SCREAM is the second book by John Dean to feature DCI Jack Harris. Be sure to check out DEAD HILL, the first book, and TO DIE ALONE, the third.

Chapter one

As the light started to fade over the northern hills, Josh Fellows stood silently in front of the old mill house and stared out at the garden, across the neatly-manicured lawn with its clipped edges to the ragged and bare trees of the copse, then through to the dark waters and the weather-beaten rowing boat moored up alongside the wooden jetty. It was a scene that he knew well and, if he squinted, he could just make out in the half-light the places where he had dug the graves. Seven of them clustered round the edges of the small lake, none of them marked, none of them tended, none of them discovered, all of them hidden among the reeds.

Seven bodies cold and lifeless in graves that no one else knew existed, each one containing a woman who was mourned and missed by loved ones but whose fate remained a mystery to all but Josh Fellows. He was the man who snatched away their young lives in moments of brutal savagery, moments of, and he had thought long and hard about the use of the word, madness. No other word would do. The thought gave him pleasure, a sense of power, and he smiled slightly as his eyes roamed the lakeside, drinking in its bleak serenity. This is what they died for. It was what he lived for. And there would be more to come. Of that he was certain. He could feel the urge to kill rising within him once more.

As he stood and stared, he heard the faint strains of violins carried on the night air as the ghosts came out to play in the half-light of dusk; he saw them rising up from the graves and dancing across the lawn, young girls tripping towards him in their brightly-coloured dresses, innocent virgins until they fell into his clutches. Now they laughed with joy, cried out with delight, their eyes full of life as they swirled and pirouetted, dancing for him. Always for him. And only for him.

Gradually, though, they faded from sight with the last vestiges of winter daylight, as did Josh's smile, and he was left staring out over a cold, empty garden as night laid its hand hard and heavy on the North Pennines valley and the first signs of frost glistened on the grass.

Josh felt the pressure of night falling in the hills; he always had, ever since he was a young boy. He remembered how his parents had sent him to the school psychiatrist at the age of seven because they were so alarmed at his nightmares. The psychiatrist had suggested that it might have been a reaction to living in a remote shepherd's cottage high on the hills. It was why his mother moved them down into the village. She had thought that being among people might help, but the nightmares did not stop.

There may have been something in their reasoning, thought Josh. There was certainly something about darkness in the hills that those who had not experienced it simply could not appreciate, he thought as he stood in the fading light and recalled those sessions in the psychiatrist's humid little consulting room down in Roxham. Something about the way that it settled on the landscape like a black curtain, creating a darkness that is almost physical, darkness that you felt you could reach out to touch.

Now, as he always did at this time of day, Josh felt at its most acute the sense of isolation closing in on him and he sensed ever more strongly the rising feeling that had driven him to kill so many times, that still drove him, the need to bring another one back here to keep the others company. To keep him company. The rage always started with a stabbing pain on his forehead and, as it grew this time, it pressed so hard that Josh felt that it would force his eyeballs from their sockets. He clenched his fist so that the fingernails dug into his skin but, just like when he dug his fingernails into their young flesh, he did not notice the trickles of blood working their way across his palms.

Josh did not understand the pain, did not know the reason for the rages that overwhelmed him or for the nightmares that still shook him roughly from sleep, even though he was now in his twenties. All he knew was that it was time to dig another grave. Standing there, he heard again the faintest strains of music drifting across the northern hills. It was time to keep the dance alive.

* * *

Darkness had long since settled over the valley and, as midnight came and went, a thin mist started to move quietly across the hillside, tripping ghost-like and silent along the becks and gulleys and winding its way down silent moss-covered ravines. The dance of night on the North Pennines. The only light in the gloom came from a couple of the cottages dotted across the hillsides, faint pinpricks of yellow that rapidly disappeared as the mist muffled the scream. For anyone close enough to hear it, it was shrill enough to turn the blood.

Jenny Meynell heard it, and not for the first time. She opened the door to her cottage half way up the hillside and stood in the heavy silence, the only sound the pounding of her heart as she listened and waited for the scream to come again. But it did not come again. How could it? Peering into the gloom, she saw nothing, no movement on the hillside, no shapes moving in the darkness. Shrouded in the mist, she felt as if she was the only person alive.

After standing there for what seemed like an age, Jenny Meynell shuddered and walked back into the cottage, glancing nervously behind her and quickly double-locking the door. It always seemed as if the outside world did not exist when she closed the door, that she was somehow cushioned from its dangers, but she knew that she would not sleep that night for fear that the scream would again disturb her dreams.

Not for the first time since she had moved into the cottage several months previously, she thought of her previous life in London and her old home standing in the midst of an Edwardian terrace, surrounded by millions of people, slamming their car doors at night, laughing loudly on the way back from the pub, playing their music. Perhaps moving here *was* a mistake, she thought as she drew the curtains to close out the devils and the demons which stalked this silent land. For all that, she had quickly grown to love this place; it *had* always been her dream when she retired, to live among the hills, a passion ignited by walking holidays in the North Pennines with her parents as a child.

Standing in front of the fading embers of the fire in the cramped living room, she tried to rationalise what had happened, to pull herself together. Maybe she had imagined the scream. Dozed off in the armchair. She *had* had a couple of glasses of red earlier in the evening. Perhaps she had heard the shriek in that netherworld between wakefulness and alcohol-fuddled sleep? On the other hand, perhaps her friends *were* right, thought Jenny as she crouched in front of the fire, stoking it to breathe new life into the flames and reaching to throw on another log from the wicker basket. They had not understood the reasons behind her move to a remote location. How could they? It had all happened so quickly. She had told them one day, left the next.

Perhaps, she thought as the coal crackled with renewed vigour, this was the wrong place after all. Perhaps she *was* just a townie with a romanticised ideal of life in the country but one incapable of actually making the change. A woman whose urban mind simply could not handle the unique challenges of rural isolation. Ok for a holiday, yes, sure, but to *live*?

Sitting in the half-light of the cottage as the clock ticked loudly on the mantelpiece, Jenny Meynell felt a long way from home and the tears began to flow. She cried in fear of the killer on the hills and in fear for the way her dream of a rural life was crumbling around her. And above all, she cried for the one thing she had always sought to escape and found herself yearning for: the sound of drunken revellers winding their noisy way home.

* * *

Josh Fellows had picked that night's victim carefully. He had watched the young girl from the shadows as she made her way home along the empty country road. Jesus, he thought, did they not listen? Did they not take note of police warnings that young women should not walk alone late at night when people like him stalked the land? The police were worried, they *must* be, and if these women ignored what was being said, they deserved everything they got, thought Josh. If it was not him who slaughtered them, it would be someone else.

It was something about the smile that had attracted him to this one. It was not always the smile; sometimes it was the hair, sometimes the curve of a waist or the swelling of young breasts. But no, with this one it was the smile. The way it lit up her face and the way it twisted into bulging-eyed fear as he tightened his grip round her neck. She had fought, silently, desperately, for the best part of two minutes but in the end he was too strong for her. He was always too strong for them and eventually the light in her eyes had dimmed and the life spirit had been quelled as she went limp in his arms.

When it was done, Josh did not look into her eyes. He did not like doing that when he violated them. Did not like staring into the lifeless pools. No, he would rather remember her as she was. Besides, he knew that her life-force would return when she danced on the lawn for him and him alone.

* * *

It was just past three in the morning and the mist was thinning when the stolen silver Audi with the fake plates drew to a halt just past the village of Carperby, one of the villages strung out along the main road through the valley. The driver cut the engine and the three occupants peered out, just able to make out a bungalow set back from the road. The house was in darkness but a porch light illuminated the driveway, allowing them to see it.

'What about that one?' said the man in the back seat. A Scouser.

'Not sure,' said the driver. A Londoner. He screwed up his eyes. 'Why is it always so sodding dark up here? The place looks a bit rundown to me.'

'They're the best, mate,' said the Scouser. 'Probably be some old dodderers who keep their jewellery in the bread bin and go to bed after Countdown.'

'Well, whatever we do,' said the driver, 'make it quick. I'm not sure we can risk a third night up here. The cops will be getting suspicious.'

The man in the passenger seat, another Londoner, frowned.

'Not sure I want to go back empty-handed,' he said.

'So let's do this place,' said the Scouser, gesturing to the bungalow. 'Looks good to me.'

'Go on then, take a look,' said the driver, 'but make it quick.'

The others got out of the car and walked up the drive. On reaching the bungalow, the Scouser forced a side window and, within seconds, had squeezed through and opened the front door to let his accomplice in. Sitting in the car, the driver could see the flash of torchlights as they searched the living room. As the minutes dragged on, he grew more nervous and started drumming his fingers on the steering wheel.

'Come on,' he murmured. 'Come on.'

He had not wanted to come north. Had never been north before and he had no intention of doing so again. More used to London and the Home Counties, he had felt ill at ease in the hills ever since they had arrived and checked into a Bed and Breakfast in Roxham before working their way up to Levton Bridge and the villages along the valley. By day, they had tried to keep a low profile as they searched for good targets but the driver had been unnerved by the way people reacted suspiciously to his questions in his London accent; the girl in the café had even commented that he was 'not from round here.' Where the Londoner came from, no one even looked at you and he found all the attention disturbing. More than anything, though, he had struggled to come to terms with the oppressive silence of the night and he hated every minute of it. That, and the flat northern beer.

He had also grown to hate the Scouser, who was only there because the front seat passenger had met him in prison a few months previously and remembered him talking about the North Pennines, the Liverpudlian beguiling his cell-mate with talk of big houses full of expensive antiques, high-end jewellery and a small police force stretched way beyond its capabilities. Big joke that had turned out to be, thought the driver gloomily as he leaned on the steering wheel and continued to watch the pinpricks of light in the bungalow.

The previous night, they had tried to burgle two farmhouses down at the bottom end of the valley but on both occasions had been disturbed by barking dogs and had fled, running to the car fearful lest they hear the panting of the pursuing animals. More than once, the driver had insisted that the break-ins were too risky but the

Scouser had brooked no opposition to his demands. Tonight had been no better than the other nights. After discounting several remote houses, they had finally given up and were heading back to Levton Bridge when they chanced across the bungalow.

The driver's bleak reverie was disturbed by the scrape of feet on the drive and he saw his accomplices scurrying towards the car; the Scouser was carrying a small box and had a triumphant look on his face.

'Bingo,' he said, getting into the back seat and opening the box to reveal four bracelets and a couple of rings, illuminated by the light of his torch. 'I got a mate on The Wirral can fence these for us.'

The driver reached back for the box and peered in.

'This is shit!' he exclaimed, hurling the box onto the back seat. 'This trip has been a fucking disaster from start to finish.'

Before the Scouser could reply, the lights went on in the house and the front door swung opened to reveal an elderly man, all wispy white hair and striped pyjamas, glaring at the car and clutching a poker. He started walking purposefully down the drive towards them, illuminating his way with a torch held in his other hand, and as he neared the vehicle he raised the poker in a threatening manner. The driver cursed, turned on the ignition and slammed the car into first, sending the wheels spinning as he jammed his foot onto the accelerator, showering the gatepost with small stones. He, for one, had had enough of the northern hills.

Chapter two

'It's nothing to worry about, madam,' said the uniformed sergeant patiently, looking across the counter at the grey-haired woman who was staring anxiously back at him out of strained and bloodshot eyes. 'Really it isn't.'

'But I tell you,' said Jenny Meynell insistently, 'it was an awful scream and I've heard it before. Last night was not the first time.'

'I'm sure it wasn't.'

After a largely sleepless night, Jenny had found her resolve strengthened and she had driven the five miles into the North Pennines hill town of Levton Bridge to report a murder. After parking her Fiat in the market square as the church clock tolled nine, she walked quickly down the hill to the Victorian building that housed the police station. Now, she stood and stared expectantly at the desk sergeant, frustrated that he did not seem to be taking her seriously. This would not have happened in London, she thought. He had not even jotted down her name.

'So what are you going to do about it?' she said.

'Do?' The officer appeared surprised by the question. 'What do you mean do?'

'Well, if a woman has been attacked…'

'With all due respect, madam, I very much doubt that she…'

'Just because we are in the countryside, it does not mean that these things do not happen,' said Jenny. 'Crime happens in rural areas as well, you know.'

'Is that a fact?'

'I tell you, it was a woman screaming and the least you can do is take it seriously.'

'You're not from around these parts, are you?'

The sergeant spoke as if to a small child and Jenny, who had used that voice many times herself during her time as a teacher at a primary school, bridled at the tone. She detested being spoken down to and the police officer's attitude infuriated her. That he looked at her almost sympathetically infuriated her even more.

'Don't you patronise me,' she said. 'I have come here in good faith and I expect you to treat me with more respect. Too many people around here seem to think that being from the south is something to be ashamed of.'

'I did not mean to offend you,' said the officer, trying to sound apologetic, mindful of the chief constable's recent memo followed by an ever sterner one from the divisional commander, after an inspection report had criticised the station's standards of customer service. 'It's just that your accent suggested…'

'I'm from London, yes, although quite what's that has got to do with anything I do not know. Besides, our streets are full of foxes. We know what they are.'

'I was only going to say, madam,' said the desk sergeant, in what he hoped was a more respectful tone, 'that if you had lived here a bit longer, you would know that what you heard last night was nothing more than a vixen.'

'A vixen?' She stared at him in disbelief. 'A bloody vixen?'

'Yes, a female fo…'

'I know what it is, man!' Images of the tattered poster which had hung on her classroom wall for many years flashed into her mind. 'I just struggle to believe that a fox could make a sound like that.'

'Lots of folks think that, but vixens have a heck of a set of lungs on them and they're very active this time of year.' The desk sergeant was on more solid ground now and he warmed to his theme. 'Early winter's the start of their breeding season, see. Noisy baskets are vixens, when they're in the mood.'

'But this sounded like someone screaming.' Her voice was smaller now. Less sure of itself. She was beginning to realise how ridiculous she must appear to this grizzled North-countryman. 'I hardly slept after I heard it last night. It sounded like someone being murdered.'

'They do sound like that.' He chuckled. 'I remember the first time I heard one, when I were a nipper. Scared the bejesus out of me, but they're harmless are vixens. Unless you're a chicken, of course.'

'Yes, but…'

'More afraid of us, are foxes, especially if we're wearing red, riding a horse and blowing a horn.' The desk sergeant hoped that the introduction of levity would ease her concerns so that she would leave him to his paperwork. She looked dubiously at him and he gave a reassuring nod. 'Might I suggest you think no more about it, Mrs…?'

'Meynell. Jenny Meynell. And it's Miss. I'm divorced.'

He jotted the name down on the pad, hoping it would help.

'Well, Miss Meynell,' he said, 'why not pop back up into the market place and have a nice cup of coffee in Mary's? She's open Mondays in winter and she does a mean fruit scone. I know that because my missus makes them for her.'

Jenny hesitated.

'I feel a bit foolish,' she said, her determination wavering in the face of his reassurance. 'I mean, I really thought... that is... I...'

'You wouldn't be the first, it's nowt to be ashamed of.' He nodded towards the door. 'Go on, love, go and get that coffee. And don't you go feeling foolish neither, you'll learn our ways soon enough. It just takes time.'

As she reached the door, he spoke again.

'Oh, Miss Meynell.'

She turned and looked at him suspiciously.

'Yes?'

'If any of the locals give you gyp about being from the south you just tell them that Sergeant Grimshaw will have their guts for garters.'

She did not reply and walked out of the door and down the steps before heading up the hill in the direction of the market place.

'Vixen's scream,' said the sergeant, shaking his head. 'Bloody southerners.'

He chuckled and picked up the desk phone.

'Jack?' he said into the receiver. 'It's that time of year again.'

Call made, the desk sergeant picked up his pen and, still chuckling, returned to his paperwork.

* * *

Upstairs in his office, Detective Chief Inspector Jack Harris, strong-jawed, thick brown hair without a hint of grey, replaced the telephone on its receiver and grinned across the desk at Matty Gallagher, a decade younger, smaller, stocky, black hair starting to thin, a man, some said, with the appearance of a monk.

'And what's tickled you?' asked the detective sergeant.

Harris was notorious for his dislike of paperwork and it was all Gallagher could do to persuade his boss to even look at the documents on the occasions when he deputised for the department's detective inspector. Left to his own devices, Harris would find any excuse to avoid the task and, once forced reluctantly to grant his sergeant an audience with the words 'twenty minutes, no more, I'm busy', it was normally done with a sour expression but his mood had lifted during the conversation with the desk sergeant.

'The Vixen's Scream,' explained Harris and, seeing his colleague's perplexed expression, added, 'surely you've heard of the Vixen's Scream?'

'This isn't bloody Midsomer Murders!' exclaimed Gallagher.

It was Harris's turn to look blank.

'Surely you've seen Midsomer Murders?' said Gallagher. 'Me and Julie love it. They've always got a fox screeching at dead of night.'

'I have no idea what you are talking about,' said Harris – there was not much room in his life for television.

'Then I must assume that it's another of your twee northern tales.'

'More an urban myth,' said Harris, his good mood meaning that he did not take offence to the comment. He took a sip of his tea from his mug. 'You know, like the one where a bloke wakes up after a night on the bevvy only to find that he's lying in the middle of a playing field and has a massive scar across his gut. Gets himself to a doctor who tells him that he's had one of his kidneys removed?'

Gallagher nodded. He'd come across the story himself during his time in the Met. The incident had happened during Gallagher's days in uniform and he'd been on desk duty in Bermondsey late one night when a dishevelled young man, who clearly had been drinking, came in and blurted out the story, claiming wide-eyed that he'd heard it in the pub and demanding that the police track down the victim to see if he was alright. Gallagher had said he would and jotted down the man's name next to the letters NFA. He was asked to tell the story to colleagues more times than he could remember in the days that followed. They'd all heard it before but it always bore the re-telling.

'So what does this one say?' asked the sergeant. 'This urban myth?'

'According to those who tell the story, someone reports a blood-curdling scream in the middle of the night and swears blind that it's a woman being murdered. Of course, local folks know it's just a vixen having a bit of a yowl to attract a mate. Don't know if you've ever heard one giving voice?'

'Not me, although I was talking to a pal of mine the other day and he saw four foxes on the night shift last week.'

'I guess foxes would be good on the night shift,' said Harris, with a slight smile.

Gallagher looked uncertainly at him; two bits of levity in the same briefing with the DCI was pretty much unheard of.

'They were rooting through bin bags, apparently,' said Gallagher. 'Looking for something to eat.'

'That's uniform for you.'

'Indeed.' Three, he thought. 'Mind, my mate didn't mention anything about a scream.'

'He would if he'd heard it, take it from me, Matty lad. It chills you to the marrow, especially if you hear it out on the hills at night like I've done a few times with the dogs.'

The inspector glanced over at the radiator, next to which lay Scoot, his black Labrador and the detective's more recent acquisition from a local animal sanctuary, a scruffy Collie by the name of Archie. Both were curled up and asleep.

'Anyway,' continued Harris, taking another gulp from his mug and returning to his story, 'the police laugh the scream off at first but when they finally relent and search the area. What do they find but a woman's body in a freshly dug grave? Of course, it's all cobblers and, just like the man and his kidneys, there is no record of anything like that ever having happened in these parts, or anywhere else for that matter, as far as I know.'

'But the story keeps cropping up?'

'It does resurface from time to time, yes. Always from townies, oddly enough.'

'Hey, less of that,' protested Gallagher, who had reluctantly moved north when his wife persuaded him that she wanted to return home and took a nursing job at the general hospital at the bottom of the valley in Roxham.

'You wait until you hear it, that's all I'm saying.' Harris picked up a piece of paper from the desk. 'Now, enough of this chit-chat. This burglary out at Carperby, what do we know?'

'They got into the bungalow sometime after three. Forced a side window. Belongs to an elderly couple. Jim and Marjorie Garbutt.'

'I know them,' nodded Harris. 'They used to farm over at Bellerby but gave it up when it got too much for the old feller. They hoped their son would take the farm on but he ended up going into web design. Broke Jim's heart, it did. They get much?'

'Bit of jewellery.' Gallagher knew that he would have to provide all the details, Jack Harris was not one for reading reports. 'Sentimental value mainly; two of the pieces had been in the family for generations and Marjorie had hoped to pass them onto her daughter.'

'And the old fellow reckons he saw them?' said Harris.

'Heard them in the living room. Chased them down the drive in his pyjamas, brandishing a poker, but they were already in the car so he didn't get close.'

'Just as well,' said Harris. 'Knowing Jim, he'd have lamped them if he got hold of them. Tough old bird is Jim Garbutt. Did a bit of boxing in his youth. Won a couple of tournaments, I seem to recall. No mention of a number plate?'

'Na, but I reckon they'd be false anyway. I'd lay good odds that the job was done by the same lot that tried to screw that house down near Roxham the night before. According to Denny, at their nick there's been reports of a couple of Londoners and a Scouser in the area the last couple of days. Anyhow, there's no sign of the car so, hopefully, the thin pickings will have persuaded them to go back home.'

'There'll be others. There'll always be others.'

Gallagher nodded; he'd seen the stats, knew that more than half the detected burglaries in the valley over the previous three years had been committed by travelling criminals from outside the area. The detectives talked for a further five minutes, working their way down the list of crimes reported overnight in the area until there was a light knock on the door and a uniformed constable walked into the office.

'You heard then?' he said, grinning at the DCI. 'Another mad-woman reporting the Vixen's Scream.'

'How do you know about it?'

'It's all over the station. You know Charlie Grimshaw, he couldn't wait to tell folks. It's given everyone a right laugh, I tell you. Bloody townies, eh?'

Gallagher pursed his lips. 'Hope this isn't the way you deal with all incomers,' he said.

Seeing Gallagher's look, the constable held up a hand.

'No offence meant, Sarge,' he said. 'Besides, you're practically one of us now. Another twenty years and you'll be like family.'

'Heap insult upon insult, why don't you?' muttered Gallagher.

'So you going to do anything about it, Jack?' grinned the constable. 'If Curtis gets to hear about it, he's bound to want it checking out. You know what he's been like since the chief's memo.'

'You leave Curtis to me,' said Harris. 'Besides, it'll blow over quickly enough. Come tomorrow, this woman will have forgotten all about it.'

* * *

The next morning, the same desk sergeant was on duty when a frightened-looking Jenny Meynell walked into the police station.

'Mrs Meynell,' said the sergeant, 'what a surprise.'

'Miss Meynell, it's Miss Meynell.'

'Of course it is, I do apologise. What can I do for you?'

'I heard it again,' she said. 'Last night. The scream.'

'But I told you it was a…'

'I don't believe you. It sounded like a woman being murdered.' She crossed her arms. 'And if you won't take me seriously, I demand to talk to someone who will.'

Charlie Grimshaw reached for the telephone. 'I'll see if one of the lads and lasses is…'

'I don't want to see some underling.'

'Yes, but…'

'Who's in charge round here?'

* * *

Josh Fellows finished filling in the grave on the edge of the lake – he loved the smell of freshly-turned earth – then stood back to admire his handiwork. He nodded with satisfaction. Neat job. No one would even know that it was there. Not that many people came here anyway. That was the beauty of the place.

Standing among the trees on the edge of the garden, Josh looked back across the lawn to the stone-built house. A former water mill whose stream had long since dried up and which had fallen into disrepair after more than forty years without an occupier, the house had recently been refurbished by its new owner, a rich businessman from London who planned to use it as a retreat from his life in the city.

Not that anyone had seen him since the day he first came to view it. All the work had been carried out by local tradesmen, at a cost, some of the locals reckoned, of close to half a million pounds. Replacement roof, new windows, kitchen extension, gravel drive, double garage made of local stone. Josh had to admit that they'd made a nice job of it. The house looked beautiful in the wan light, shrouded as it was in the gentle early morning mist, a lost building miraculously brought back to life. There had been talk that the owner might try to sell it but nothing had come of it, so still it stood empty.

Josh, who had been retained as the gardener by the land agents managing the property on the owner's behalf, turned back to the grounds and let his gaze roam slowly round the fringes of the lake, pausing lovingly at the spot where each grave lay. Finally, his attention settled on the latest burial place. He wondered when someone would report her missing. He imagined the tears of a mother, husband, boyfriend and smiled: tonight there would be another girl to dance for him when dusk fell on the northern hills.

Chapter three

'Why me?' protested Harris staring bleakly across the divisional commander's desk at the tall uniformed officer with his sharply angular features and thinning, dark hair. 'I've already got a shed-load of…'

'You know why you,' said Philip Curtis with the slightest of smiles. 'Foxes are part of your job, are they not? Besides, all I'm asking you to do is pop down to the front counter to reassure her.'

There had been a time when Jack Harris would have stalked out of the office; it had not always been an easy relationship. Harris's role as a wildlife officer was only a part-time addendum to running CID in the valley but it had, over the years, turned him into a national figure much in demand to address conferences and give media interviews. When Curtis, a newly-promoted superintendent on the fast-track to high office, had arrived at Levton Bridge he made it clear that he did not like the amount of time that his divisional head of CID lavished on such affairs.

Not that the initial mutual dislike was all about wildlife; part of it was connected with one of the superintendent's first decisions on arriving at Levton

Bridge. Detesting the fact that the inspector took Scoot wherever he went, Curtis issued a memo banishing all but police dogs from divisional headquarters at Levton Bridge, a decision he was forced to reverse in the face of protests from staff, everyone from old constables to bright-faced young secretaries who had been feeding Scoot titbits for years and were later to do the same for Archie as well. Curtis had resented the loss of face but from such unpromising beginnings, the two men had gradually forged a relationship based on grudging respect.

'Foxes may well be part of my job,' grunted Harris, realising that old arguments had been adroitly turned against him by his commander, 'but mad old women banging on about murders are definitely not.'

'You've seen the chief's memo. We've got to make sure that our dealings with the public are first rate. Something like this could be very damaging if we let it run.'

'Yes, but…'

'If word gets out that she reckons that girls are being murdered by someone in the area…' The superintendent shot Harris a sly look. 'I mean, they can be a pretty unforgiving lot when it comes to outsiders, can they not? As I recall, it took a certain DCI the best part of a year to give his commander the time of day and I'd only come up the valley from Roxham. And if she takes this to the media…'

'Ok, ok, point taken, but she's a barn-pot and everyone knows it.'

'Maybe so, but folks up here can get some strange ideas into their heads.'

Reluctantly, Harris nodded. A local man by birth, he had always appreciated how claustrophobic life could be in the division's hill communities. Escaping such realities was the reason that, as a young man, he had joined the Army: to leave behind bad influences and explore the world beyond the valley's narrow horizons. Even when he left the Army and returned to civilian life, Harris had initially opted to start his police career to the south, in Manchester, rather than returning to Levton Bridge. The pull of the hills had eventually proved too strong, however, as he knew it always would, but he nevertheless accepted the posting at Levton Bridge with some reservations; he knew that a place where everyone knew everyone's business could be wearing.

'I guess you're right,' sighed the inspector, noting the commander's expectant expression. 'OK, I'll go down and see her. What's the message we want to put out?'

'Jack Harris on message?' Curtis gave another smile. 'What on earth is the world coming to? You'll be reading my memos next. Just make sure that she stops this nonsense. I am sure you will find a diplomatic form of words with your new enlightened approach to community relations.'

Harris stood up. 'I'm sure I will,' he said.

He had just left the office when Matty Gallagher rushed down the corridor towards him, pulling on his coat as he did so.

'Where's the fire?' asked Harris.

'Jim Garbutt, the old fellow who disturbed the gang screwing his bungalow? The surgery has just been on. He'd come in with chest pains and collapsed in the doctor's room. Sounds like a coronary. They're waiting for an ambulance. I'm off there now.'

'I know his wife,' said Harris. 'I'll go with…'

'No he won't,' said the commander's voice from his office. 'He's got to see someone at the front counter about a sex-starved fox!'

Gallagher could not conceal his smile. Nor did he try to. Harris scowled.

'Oh, and Matthew,' shouted the commander, appearing at his office door as the sergeant headed for the stairs, 'keep me posted on what happens with Jim Garbutt.'

* * *

A couple of minutes later, Gallagher was running across the market place, arriving at the surgery as two ambulance officers carried Jim Garbutt out on a stretcher, followed by his weeping wife supported by one of the receptionists. The sergeant glanced down at the old man as he passed by; his eyes were closed, his skin grey, his breathing shallow. Gallagher had seen dying people before, too many for his liking, and knew that it did not look good.

His mind was also taking in the potential ramifications. He knew only too well how something like this could ferment feeling among the close-knit communities of the valley. A small crowd had already gathered to watch in solemn silence and, as the ambulance pulled away to begin its journey down the valley to Roxham, its siren blaring, the blue lights on, Gallagher heard mutterings and noticed one or two people glancing in his direction.

'Should string them up,' said a middle-aged woman in what the sergeant assumed to be intended for him to hear. 'They should stay where they belong.'

There were murmurs of agreement from the crowd. Gallagher resisted the temptation to say something, contenting himself with a sour look in their direction, and instead turned on his heel and stalked into the surgery where a young woman was standing with a man in his thirties.

'You must be Ellie,' said the sergeant, still trying to control his irritation at the crowd's comments. 'Thank you for calling us.'

'I guessed you'd be interested, knowing that he'd only just been burgled.'

Gallagher nodded. 'Definitely a heart attack?' he asked.

The receptionist glanced at the tall dark-haired man in his thirties standing next to her.

24

'Dr Hailes is the one to ask about that,' she said.

'Yeah, heart attack, I reckon,' said the doctor with a nod. 'I'd only just started examining him when he collapsed. His heart rate was all over the place. Lucky it happened here. We've got a defibrillator. If it had happened at his home he'd have been a goner, for sure.'

'So he'll live then?' asked the sergeant, the vision of the old man's pallid face still at the forefront of his mind.

'I wouldn't bet on it even if you gave me the money,' said John Hailes. 'Sorry, I know it's not what you want to hear.'

'Do you think it was brought on by the shock of the break-in?'

'Jim's had a bad heart for several years. It's why he gave up the farm. Plus, he is seventy-seven. Could have happened any time but disturbing those burglars will not have done him any good. His wife said he had been agitated about it.'

Gallagher looked at him gloomily. The death of a much-loved local with the blame falling on outsiders would be a potent cocktail, Gallagher knew that, just as he also knew that for all the communities of the valley tended to be peaceable for the most part, age-old tensions were never far below the surface. Most people accepted outsiders, welcomed them, embraced them into community life, but some did not and the detective sergeant knew that it did not take much to ignite strong emotions.

A thought struck him.

'Your accent,' he said to the doctor. 'You're not from round here, are you?'

'I'm from Nottingham but my wife had to come home to be nearer her mother after her father died. She works at the solicitors in the market place. I didn't mind, to be honest, me and Annie used to come up here mountain biking whenever we could anyway.'

'The locals give you any trouble since you arrived?' asked the sergeant. 'I mean, for being from away?'

'Not really. The odd one plays up.'

'So what do you do when that happens?'

The doctor smiled.

'I sent the last one for a rectal scan,' he said.

* * *

'And what rank are you?' asked Jenny Meynell as the inspector bade her sit down at the table in the interview room situated off the reception area. She looked suspiciously at his suit. 'I expected a proper policeman.'

'Ah, the glamour of uniform,' said Harris. 'Actually, I'm a detective chief inspector. Head of CID for the division.'

'A detective? Then you're taking me seriously?' she said, sitting down and looking triumphantly at him. 'Well, I am glad someone around here is. That fool of a man on the desk seemed to think that I was some sort of mad-woman. He was extremely patronising.'

'I am also a wildlife liaison officer,' said Harris, sitting down opposite her.

Her bright expression faded.

'Wildlife liaison officer?' she said in a hollow voice. 'Animals?'

'I am afraid so. Look, Miss Meynell, you are not going to like what I am about to say. I know the desk sergeant is not the most tactful of human beings but I do think that he is right. What you are hearing is a vixen. Lots of people mistake it for a human screaming. You're not the first person to have done it and you won't be the last.'

'Just because before this I lived in Redbridge…' She hesitated. It seemed to the inspector that she regretted saying it but he was not sure why. She recovered quickly. 'Anyway, that's beside the point. I know what I heard, Chief Inspector.' She gave him a hard stare. 'I heard a woman being attacked.'

'No, you didn't.'

'But…'

'Look, Miss Meynell, this has got to stop and stop now,' said Harris firmly. Chief constable's memo or not, the inspector resolved to bring an end to the situation. 'You're making yourself look foolish.'

'How dare you speak to me like that?' she said. 'This would not happen in London. They are more professional down there. You could learn a lot from them.'

Gallagher's face flashed into the inspector's mind. Bloody Chirpies, he thought.

'Listen,' said Harris, 'folks round here are already hacked off that most of our crime is committed by people from outside the area. How do you think they will react now that you are suggesting that one of them may be murdering women? You'll just bring trouble down on your head, which makes no sense when you've only just moved into the area.'

She did not respond immediately but considered his words for a few moments. In the heavy silence of the interview room, her demeanour changed. She seemed somehow smaller.

'There have already been comments,' she said eventually, the belligerence draining away.

'Comments? What kind of comments?'

'The first one came a month or so after I moved into my cottage. A man came to the door. Asked if I wanted to buy any eggs and when I said no… Well, suffice to say he called me a Cockney something. I may have been a bit rude to him myself.'

'Get away. Oh, don't look like that. You have to admit that you're not exactly the most diplomatic of people.'

She looked as if she was about to argue the point then seemed to change her mind and said nothing.

'You get a name for this man?' asked Harris.

She shook her head.

'A description then?' he asked.

'Scruffy. Long brown hair. Did not look like it had been washed for a long time. He wore a tatty denim jacket with badges down the arms. Oh, and he was driving an old car. Lots of scratches on the paintwork.'

'Blue?'

'Yes, not that you could tell through all the dirt. Do you know who it was?'

'Yes, he's one of our scroats,' nodded the inspector. 'I'll have a word. That the only incident with him?'

'No. A few days later I was coming out of the Co-op when I saw him again, with some of his friends. Near one of the market place pubs. They shouted something at me, I did not quite hear it but I don't think it was pleasant. I have seen him a few times since and he always gives me an ugly look.' She seemed close to tears. 'This is not what I thought it would be like.'

'And what did you think it would be like?'

'I don't know.' She looked at him unhappily. 'It's such a beautiful area, I thought that the people would be more… welcoming, I suppose. Was I wrong?'

'There's folks living here that have hardly ever left the valley.' The detective's tone was softer now. 'They're ok once you get to know them.'

'I suppose it could have been a fox.'

'I am sure it was. Go on,' said Harris, standing up. 'Pop up into the market place and have a nice cup of coffee. Mary's is open, she does a nice scone.'

Jenny Meynell gave a slight smile, the first time she had smiled since entering the room.

'Are you on commission as well?' she said.

He looked puzzled.

'Your desk sergeant,' she explained. 'His wife makes the scones.'

They walked out into reception where Harris watched her head for the door. She paused with her hand on the handle and turned back to look at him.

'What if you find a body, Chief Inspector?' she said.

'What?' The question took him by surprise.

'What if you find a body?' she repeated.

'I am sure we won't.'

'Let's hope not.'

She pushed her way through the door and walked down the steps. When she had gone, Harris glanced at the desk sergeant, who shook his head and continued with his paperwork.

'Off her rocker, that one,' he said.

'I guess,' said the inspector.

He went outside to stand at the top of the steps, where he thoughtfully watched Jenny Meynell walk briskly up the hill in the direction of the market place. Half way up, she passed Gallagher who was on his way back down towards the police station having left the doctor's surgery. The officer had an angry expression on his face.

'What news?' asked Harris as the sergeant reached the police station and walked up the steps towards his boss.

'Fucking woolly-backs,' replied Gallagher.

'That's the spirit,' said Harris.

* * *

Josh Fellows finished digging the border and leaned against his spade. Breathing hard from his exertions, he wiped the sweat from his brow and glanced around the garden. The clock on the gable end of the mill house chimed eleven, sounding out the hours in slow sonorous beats. He smiled. Soon it would be killing time again.

Chapter four

'But why so bothered?' asked Gallagher as he and Harris walked up the hill from the police station, the sharp sun casting shadows on the pavement. 'I thought you said that Curtis was being paranoid about this Meynell woman.'

'Maybe he is,' replied the inspector, 'but the last thing we want is new people coming into the area and being abused by the locals.'

'I didn't think you cared that much,' said Gallagher as they turned the corner into the market place. 'You did not exactly make me feel welcome when I first arrived.'

'Exactly, Matty lad. Abusing new people is my job and I don't like it when other people muscle in on my territory. Besides, you'd have been alright if you hadn't kept telling us how they did things better in the Met. The last thing us woolly-backs want is to be told that we're woolly-backs. Especially by Cockney wide-boys.'

'Ok, ok,' said Gallagher, holding his hands up in surrender. 'Point taken.'

'Besides,' continued the inspector as they walked round the corner, into the market place and past the Co-op, 'what with this bloody memo from the Chief, the last thing we want is our Miss Meynell bleating on to headquarters that we're ignoring her complaint. Her type of busy-body can cause no end of bother.'

'Makes sense, I guess. Where we going to look for Lenny Mattocks then?'

Harris glanced at the clock in the middle of the square.

'Eleven,' he said. 'My money is on the King's Head.'

'Me, too,' said Gallagher as they crossed the market place and headed for the rundown pub. 'Low Life Central, that is.'

'Indeed,' said Harris, pushing his way through the front door and wrinkling his nose at the musty smell from the threadbare carpets. 'Jesus, Ray, I hope that's not your Meryl's cooking.'

Standing behind the bar, the landlord stopped wiping the beer glass and eyed him without enthusiasm; he had little time for Jack Harris and his team. There was only one customer in the lounge, a scruffy unshaven young man with unkempt brown hair who leaned against the bar, nursing a pint of bitter. He was wearing a threadbare denim jacket and trousers with holes in the knees. The detectives eyed Lenny Mattocks with distaste. Lenny Mattocks, for his part, eyed them with suspicion as they walked over to him.

'What do you want?' muttered Mattocks, who had a string of minor offences to his name, 'I ain't done nothing wrong.'

'I'm sure that's not true, Lenny,' said Harris. 'However, we're actually here to present you with an award.'

'An award?' said Mattocks. 'What kind of award?'

'From the tourist board,' said Harris. 'For being welcoming to people from outside the area. It's a new initiative.'

Mattocks looked confused.

'You've been causing me grief, Lenny boy,' said Harris, his voice hardening, 'and as you well know, I don't like people who cause me grief.'

Mattocks looked worried. He did know. The inspector's reputation had been hard-earned and Lenny Mattocks had the bruises to prove it.

'How'd I cause you grief?' asked Mattocks. 'I ain't done nothing to hack you off, Mr Harris. Honest.'

'Actually, you have. You've been upsetting Miss Meynell and she's been bending my ear about it.'

'Never heard of her.'

'The woman from the cottage above Carperby,' said Harris. 'Seems you gave her a mouthful when she wouldn't buy your eggs. I say, your eggs, what odds that if we look a bit closer we'll discover that they were nicked? Old Bob Gent has been saying for months that someone is raiding his coops and unless the foxes have learnt to use wire-cutters, I reckon you're in the frame for it.'

Mattocks looked even more worried.

'So,' said Harris, 'remember our Miss Meynell now?'

'Mebbese. She were rude to me. She said if she wanted eggs she'd go to the supermarket. Fucking Cockneys.'

'Hey, hey,' said Gallagher quickly. 'Less of your mouth.'

Mattocks looked alarmed.

'I didn't mean you, Mr Gallagher,' he said quickly. 'You're practically one of us now, you are.'

'You're the second person that has said that to me today,' grunted Gallagher. 'And I didn't like it when the first one said it either.'

'Anyway, Lenny,' said Harris, putting an arm on his shoulder and giving it a squeeze that made the bones crack. 'I want you to behave yourself from now on. Treat Jenny Meynell like she's the Queen of England. Last thing I want is having to waste time because of your antics. I've got enough to do without that. Understand?'

Mattocks nodded and the detectives left the pub, ignoring the sour look from the landlord. Having passed the Co-op again, the inspector stopped walking and glanced in through the window of the tearoom to see Jenny Meynell sitting alone, hunched over a cup of tea and a half-eaten scone. She noticed the inspector and waved.

'I'll catch you up later,' said Harris. 'Going to see my new best pal.'

'Rather you than me.'

As Gallagher disappeared round the corner, the inspector entered the tearoom, a jingling bell announcing his arrival. Harris sat down opposite Jenny Meynell.

'I've talked to Lenny Mattocks,' he said. 'The man who abused you. You'll have no more bother from him.'

'Thank you.'

'No problem.' The inspector stood up, shaking his head at the young waitress who had started walking towards him, order pad in hand. He patted his stomach. 'No thanks, Ally, I haven't digested the last fruit scone yet. Your aunt using concrete mix again?'

Ally grinned and went back behind the counter. Harris walked over to the door and Jenny Meynell waited until he had reached for the handle before she spoke.

'I'm not crazy, you know,' she said. 'About the scream. It was a woman.'

'I'm sure you think so,' said Harris, turning back towards her.

'Exactly how sure are you, Chief Inspector?'

Jack Harris did not reply. The bell tinkled again as he headed out into the street and walked round the corner onto the hill, deep in thought. If the inspector was honest with himself, Jenny Meynell did not look like the kind of person to make things up – and certainly not the deranged mad-woman portrayed in the descriptions proffered by others. No, she may be a townie unused to country ways but the conviction behind her words had him troubled and he did not know why. He quickened his stride and caught up with his sergeant almost at the police station.

'Wait a minute, Matty lad,' said Harris as they reached the bottom of the steps.

Gallagher stopped and surveyed his boss, intrigued by the expression on his face. One he had not seen before. Uncertain. Uneasy. Lacking in its usual confidence.

'What's up with you?' asked the sergeant. 'She give you a hard time again?'

'Look, don't let this get around,' said Harris in a low voice even though the street was deserted. 'People will think I've gone mad.'

'Who'd dare tell you?' Gallagher noticed the serious expression on his boss's face. 'What's the big secret anyway?'

'What if Jenny Meynell is right?'

'But you said she was a loony. You said that us southern softies would not know a fox if it came up and…'

'I know what I said. Look, do a check, will you? See if we've got any missing women reports that…'

'I can tell you now that we haven't.'

'How do you know?'

'OK,' sighed Gallagher, 'time to fess up. Something about her story disturbed me as well so I did some checking. Just on the computer, nobody knows I did it.'

'It's not just me lost control of my senses then?' said Harris as they crossed the police station reception area.

'Seems not,' said Gallagher, as they walked through another door and up the stairs to the first floor. 'But there's no one. Nothing in other forces that links back to us either.'

'Just as I thought.' Harris gave his sergeant a satisfied look. 'It's a hollering fox, plain and simple, and Jenny Meynell is going to have to accept it sometime.'

'Not sure she'll do that,' said Gallagher as they reached the top of the steps and headed in different directions, Harris towards his office, the sergeant to the squad room.

'End of story, though,' said Gallagher over his shoulder.

'End of story indeed,' replied Harris.

However, it wasn't the end of the story for Jack Harris and the conversation nagged away at the inspector for the rest of the day as he went about his business. Throughout two meetings, one with the divisional commander about staffing budgets and one with some earnest-looking people from Neighbourhood Watch who wanted to talk about shed burglaries, the detective chief inspector found his mind wandering more than it usually did on such occasions.

Four o'clock found him sitting at his desk, trying desperately to focus on the latest missives from headquarters but repeatedly walking over to the window, past the dogs lying beneath the radiator, and staring out of the window and down into the police yard. Eventually, he cursed, threw the document he was reading onto the desk, eliciting startled looks from the dogs, and picked up the desk phone. He dialled an outside number.

'Leckie,' said a familiar voice on the other end.

A uniformed constable with Greater Manchester Police, Graham Leckie was one of the inspector's closest friends, the two men having met some years previously when Harris worked for the force. Initially they had connected through their shared love of wildlife but, after Harris had moved north to Levton Bridge, they talked regularly for another reason. Graham Leckie worked in force intelligence and because the Levton Bridge area regularly witnessed crimes committed by criminals coming into the area from further south the exchange of information between the two men had proved invaluable.

'It's Hawk,' said the inspector.

'Hawk, good to hear from you.' Only the inspector's closest friends called him Hawk and there was genuine delight in Leckie's voice. 'High time we organised another fishing trip, I reckon.'

'Sounds good,' said Harris. 'I was up at one of the pools the other day with the dogs and there were plenty of grayling around. Talking of fishing, I need a favour. You still working on that national database of missing persons?'

'Sure am. Even a Luddite like you can tap into it, you know. You don't need me.'

'Yeah, but this is not a straightforward one. I am probably looking for someone who does not exist.'

'Your faith in the capacity of the software is touching. What you after, old son?'

'Soft intelligence that links missing women from outside our force area to this neck of the woods.'

'But you don't have any names?'

'Like I said, I don't even know if they exist. I don't really want to elaborate at this stage, partly because it could make me look stupid.'

'Who would dare tell you?'

'You're the second person who's said that today.'

'Bet the other one was Matty Gallagher,' chuckled Leckie.

'Yeah, it was. Listen, Matty is the only other person in on this and I'd appreciate it if it stayed that way.'

'Sure.'

Jack Harris replaced the receiver, sighed and sat back in his chair. An image of Jenny Meynell's defiant face flashed into his mind.

'Bloody woman has got me at it now,' he grunted.

He glanced at the wall clock, then out of the window. Noting the fading afternoon light, the inspector walked across the office, watched in anticipation by the dogs. Harris reached his Barbour jacket down from the peg on the back of the door.

'Come on,' he said. 'I've had enough of today.'

* * *

Five minutes later, telephone to his ear, Matty Gallagher stood at the window of the CID room and looked down at the yard.

'Yes, I'll hold,' said the sergeant, returning his attention to Roxham General Hospital as he heard a woman's voice. 'Yes. Hello, yes, Jim Garbutt. They brought him in earlier today. Suspected heart attack. Still critical? Ok, can you let me know of any change? Thank you.'

The sergeant replaced the receiver and stared moodily out of the window for a few moments. He recalled yet again the ugly murmurings among the small crowd gathered outside the surgery as the stretcher bearing the old man was carried out to the waiting ambulance. It would help, he decided, if they could track down the three men in the car who had been spotted casing out houses in the valley but traffic seemed convinced that it had long since left the area. Gallagher tended to agree.

As the sergeant noted the rapidly darkening afternoon sky, he found himself suddenly assailed by disturbing feelings that he had experienced on more and more occasions over recent months. The sergeant sighed; he loved Julie, always had, always would, but sometimes it felt as if he had given up a lot to be with her. The sergeant had always assumed that such feelings would subside but it still did not take much to trigger them and thought of Jenny Meynell's former life had done the job this time.

'Pull yourself together, man,' he murmured.

* * *

Darkness had long since fallen over the hills once more when the first stone struck the window of Jenny Meynell's cottage. Sitting in front of the fire, half asleep from the effects of the warm fug of the room and her third glass of red wine, she started when it clattered into the glass followed by two more then, struggling to gather her senses, got to her feet and wrenched open the door. Peering out, she could not see anyone in the inky darkness but clearly heard the sound of someone running down the track, then the guttural cough of an engine as it was coaxed into life. For a long time, she watched its lights thread their way along the valley road back towards Levton Bridge before finally disappearing from view, then stood on the doorstep in the roaring silence of the night and let the tears roll hot and acrid down her cheeks. Shortly after 3am, having lain awake listening to every sound from the settling timbers of the cottage, she drifted into an uneasy sleep, which was when she heard the vixen's scream again.

* * *

Two miles to the north and sitting at home, Jack Harris fancied that he heard it, too. Home for the inspector was a remote cottage on a narrow track halfway up the local landmark, Dead Hill. Harris had purchased the building after stumbling across it while out on a walk with Scoot, loving the way that the cottage was obscured from the winding valley road below by a fold in the hillside. The former shepherd's cottage had been in a dilapidated condition and it had taken the inspector the best part of two years to restore it, doing most of the tasks himself and calling in favours for the rest. Now, it was his bolthole, close enough to Levton Bridge if he needed to get there quickly but far enough to escape the bustle of the world. He liked the fact that he could not see any other buildings from his window.

Having spent the evening sitting in front of his coal fire and sipping whisky while reading a much-thumbed book on buzzard ecology, part of his preparation for a lecture he was due to deliver at a raptor conference the following month, the inspector had only just gone to bed when he heard the scream. Or fancied that he had heard it. Hovering in the hinterland between wakefulness and sleep, he snapped to his senses.

Getting out of bed, he walked over to the window, not bothering to switch on the bedside lamp, pulled open one of the curtains and peered out into the darkness. Nothing. No light, no movement. Just blackness.

'Bloody hell,' muttered the inspector, letting the curtain flap back into place and getting back into bed, moving the dogs out of the way to make room for his large frame, 'I really am letting that woman get to me.'

* * *

Josh Fellows heard the scream as well. Standing in the darkness, he waited for the sound to stop reverberating round the hills before picking up the woman's lifeless body and beginning his long walk across the fields.

Chapter five

It was just after midnight when the two Londoners drove the silver Audi onto the wasteland in Redbridge and got out of the vehicle. While one of them kept watch, the other reached into the back and produced a petrol can. Having unscrewed the cap, he proceeded to sprinkle the paraffin liberally over the front and back seats.

'Get back,' he said and struck a match.

The two men stood and watched as the flames took hold and illuminated the night sky. A bedroom light was switched on in one of the nearby houses and a figure appeared at the window.

'Come on,' said the driver, 'let's get out of here and if anyone asks me to go up north again they can boil their head.'

* * *

Jack Harris did not normally suffer from nightmares; even when he had found himself in testing situations during his years serving with the military, he had been the envy of his comrades with his capacity to enjoy what he liked to describe as 'the sleep of the just'. Not even after facing up to heavily-armed militants in Kosovo during his stint at as military hostage negotiator had his sleep been affected. However, on this occasion, the inspector's slumber was disturbed by relentless images of his beloved hills plunged into gloom by heavy, black clouds which were closing in as he and the dogs struggled to find the right path across the moors.

Eventually, the man who knew every slope and every track of the valley better than anyone, recognised nothing and was lost. That was when he saw a figure standing on the path a hundred metres in front of him, silhouetted by a glow behind him. Peering closer, Harris could see that the man was carrying what appeared to be a body in his arms. As the shocked inspector struggled to make out the man's features, the figure threw back its head and emitted a curdling scream which reverberated round the hills.

As the panic started to rise up inside him, the inspector snapped awake and realised that the scream had been his own. Sweating profusely and with his heart pounding, he reached out to switch on the bedside lamp, which was when he noticed that the dogs were sitting up on the bed and staring at him.

'Sorry, guys,' he murmured. He reached out to pat each of them reassuringly then put out the light and lay in the darkness for a while, waiting for his heart to return to normal. 'Bloody woman. The sooner she fucks off back to London the better and I don't care who knows it.'

Having finally slipped back into a light and fitful sleep, the inspector was shaken awake again, this time by a phone call. He glanced at his digital clock; the glowing figures said that it was not yet 6.30am. Muttering a curse, and knowing that it could only be bad news at such an hour, the inspector picked up the bedside phone, his arm instantly feeling the biting chill of the cold air in the room.

'Harris,' he grunted into the receiver. 'This had better be good.'

'It's Control at Levton Bridge, Sir,' said a women's voice. 'I am really sorry to ring you, Sir, but a woman's body has been found in a field north of Carperby. A shepherd stumbled across it.'

'Carperby!' exclaimed Harris and sat bolt upright, immediately awake. 'Did you say Carperby?'

'Yes. Why?'

'Nothing. Do we know any more?'

'Sergeant Gallagher is on his way there now. Uniform are already on the scene. Sergeant Gallagher said to tell you that the woman had a head injury.'

A few minutes later, having hurriedly thrown on his clothes and bustled the dogs into the back of the Land Rover, a grim-faced Harris drove down the track leading down from his cottage, the vehicle bumping and grinding as he gunned the engine far too hard for the rough surface. Once on the main road, the inspector guided the vehicle on the short trip along the main valley road to Carperby, his thoughts racing as he did so. Please God, not Jenny Meynell, the ramifications playing out large in his mind. The media would have a field day. Jack Harris could see the headlines now and he knew that the chief constable would do the same when he heard what had happened.

Not a man normally given to doubt, the inspector ran through his dealings with Jenny Meynell time and time again, the encounter with Curtis, the conversation with the frightened women in the interview room at the police station, the brief chat in the coffee shop, trying to reassure himself that he, at least, had taken her anxiety seriously.

What if you find a body, Inspector?

Concluding that he had done all that could be reasonably expected of him, the inspector realised that the speed of the vehicle had hit eighty without him noticing and he slowed down in time to drive through the slumbering village of Carperby, the houses still in darkness, their occupants unaware of the horror unfolding nearby. As the Land Rover passed the last house, the inspector saw the flashing blue lights of two patrol cars parked on the roadside ahead of him.

Pulling onto the verge, the inspector got out and gave a hopeful look towards Jenny Meynell's cottage several hundred metres further along the slope. Desperate to see a reassuring light, her figure framed in the window, he saw only darkness and frowned.

What if you find a body, Inspector?

Well, he had. Amid the grey hues of dawn, the inspector strode across the field and, frosted grass crunching beneath his boots, headed towards Matty Gallagher, who was standing on the far side of the field, with his anorak hood turned up against the chill of the morning. The sergeant was talking to the shepherd who had found the body but broke off from his conversation, leaving a uniformed officer to continue the questioning of the shocked man.

'You look like shit,' said Gallagher, surveying the unshaven inspector.

'Crap night. You got up fast from Roxham.'

'Couldn't sleep. Never can when Julie's on nights. Came in early to catch up on paperwork and was walking past the Control room when the call came in.'

Harris gestured towards the body, which lay in the lee of the drystone wall running along the top of the field. It had been rolled into a dip in the ground and was not visible from the road.

'I hardly dare ask,' he said as the detectives started walking towards the dead woman. 'Is it…?'

'It's not Jenny Meynell, if that's what you're thinking. Not much of a solace, though.' Gallagher pointed towards the dimly visible shape of the cottage further up the hillside. 'Mind, I am pretty sure that's where she lives.'

'It is, yes,' said the inspector, coming to a halt at the corpse and looking down into the lifeless face of an attractive young blonde woman. She was wearing a bright red dress which was torn in several places. No coat and no shoes. 'God, she's young, Matty lad.'

'I know.' Gallagher gave a slight shake of the head. A veteran of many murder inquiries, most of them from his years in the Met, he knew from bitter experience that it was always toughest with the young ones. Children and teenagers, they were the ones that tore at the heartstrings most of all. All that wasted potential. Lives unlived. 'We reckoned she can only be nineteen, if that.'

The inspector nodded and turned his attention to the rips in the dress and the scratches on her arms.

'Looks like she tried to fight him off,' he said. 'Any idea who she is?'

'Afraid not. No handbag, no ID, not even a mobile phone. And no indication as to what she was doing out here either.' Gallagher gestured to the uniformed officers now taping off the entrance to the field. 'None of them recognise her.'

Harris crouched down to better examine the ugly wound on the side of the girl's head, the blood having flowed across the right cheek and dribbled down to stain her blue waterproof jacket. The wound was caked hard and Harris reached out to gently touch her face. It was like ice.

'Been here a while,' he said.

'Maybe she was trying to get back to the village,' said Gallagher, looking along the road to Carperby, now revealing itself in the pale morning gloom. The first lights were coming on in the windows. 'Maybe she was staying with someone. Or on vacation. There's a couple of holiday lets on the green.'

'Yeah, Carperby this time of year is really popular,' grunted Harris. 'So what do you think happened?'

'Gets bevvied up, tries to walk home. Loses her way in the darkness, stumbles across the field, falls, hits her head…' Gallagher noted the inspector's sceptical expression and added, acutely aware at the defensive tone in his voice. 'People do daft things when they've had a few sherbets.'

'She'd have frozen to death long before she got this far. It's been pretty cold the last few nights,' said Harris, straightening up. 'But we'd both be kidding ourselves if we believed your story. This is no accident and we both know it.'

Gallagher nodded. He had been speaking more in hope than expectation, trying to convince himself that another human being had not taken this young life. Neither man spoke for a few moments as they stared down at the girl. Both knew what the other was thinking. Gallagher's voice when it broke the silence was flat.

'Dumped then?' he said. 'Someone with a vehicle. An outsider?'

'I can't see any of the locals being capable of this.'

'Sure?'

Harris gave him a look. 'Aren't you?'

'Just asking.'

'Yes, I'm sure.'

There was another silence as Gallagher contemplated what to say next. He knew only too well how defensive Harris could be if accusations were levelled at people in the area. Gallagher also knew that the inspector always came round to the right way of thinking in the end; you just had to give him time.

'If we assume that the killer is from away,' said the sergeant, his mind going back once more to the gathering he had witnessed outside the doctor's surgery, 'we both know how that will play with the locals when word gets out.'

Harris nodded gloomily.

What if you find a body, Inspector?

Thought of Jenny Meynell prompted the inspector to look along the slope to her cottage, noting that a light had now come on in the bedroom.

'Get the team out, will you?' he said, starting to walk back across the field.

'Already on it. The DI's heading to the factory as we speak. Where are you going?' Gallagher saw the light in the cottage. 'Ah. Not so crazy now, eh?'

'It would seem not.' After a few paces, the inspector turned and gave a half smile. 'What's the Cockney rhyming slang for I told you so?'

'Not sure we have a phrase for that. I think it's because Londoners think we are always right.'

Harris flapped a hand and continued towards Jenny Meynell's cottage. She was standing at the open front door, wearing a pink dressing gown, watching the inspector walk up the muddy path.

'You've found a body, haven't you?' she said as he arrived at the doorstep.

'We have, yes.'

'I told you.'

'No special phrase, then,' murmured Harris.

'What?' She looked sharply at him.

'Nothing.'

Jenny led the way into the dimly-lit living room with its china dog ornaments on the shelves and a carriage clock above the mantelpiece. She gestured to the sofa and he sat down. Feeling the chill of the morning, Harris hoped that she would offer to make a cup of tea but she did not, instead sitting in the armchair and eying him intensely.

'Is it a murder?' she asked.

'It looks like it, yes. A young girl. Could have been there a few days.'

'Do you know who she is?'

Harris shook his head.

'You should have taken me more seriously.' Her voice was louder now, more strident. 'I have half a mind to contact your chief constable. I read what he said in the paper about improving the way you deal with members of the public and the way you and your officers…'

'Actually, I did take you seriously, Miss Meynell. More seriously than you think.'

'Not seriously enough, it would seem, though.'

Harris sighed. The woman always had an answer.

'Well, what did you expect me to do?' he said. 'Some woman wanders into the police station and…'

'Some woman? Is that how you view me? Some woman?'

'I am sorry, poor choice of words.' He tried to look apologetic but under her stern gaze all he could think of was how badly he needed a shave. 'Look at it from our point of view, for a moment, will you? You told us that you had heard a scream. Fair enough, but I checked our records and there was no one unaccounted for.'

'She's accounted for now, isn't she?' Jenny walked over to the window, drew the curtains and looked down at the police officers in the field.

Harris did not reply and Jenny continued her perusal of the scene. More police cars had arrived and officers were erecting a white tent over the body to protect it from the drizzle that had started to fall. An ambulance had parked on the main road and two green-clad paramedics were making their way across the field to a bald man in a dark anorak, who seemed to be directing affairs. Jenny turned back into the room.

'What more evidence do you need, Chief Inspector?' she asked tartly.

'I still do not think that there is any link,' snapped Harris. 'Besides, you heard the scream on a few nights and we have only found the one body.'

'What if there are others and you have not found them yet?'

Harris nodded gloomily. It was what both he and Gallagher had been thinking as they stood and stared down at the body in the field but that neither had wished to say. The possibility of a dump-site pointed to a serial killer, the two words that changed everything for all involved.

'I don't feel safe,' said Jenny quietly, coming to sit back on the armchair and looking at him. The stridency had gone to be replaced with an air of vulnerability.

'I would not worry. I am sure that you are perfectly…'

'My house was attacked last night,' she said. She nodded to three small stones on the hearth. 'Someone threw those at the windows. I'm surprised that they didn't shatter.'

Before Harris could reply, Jenny looked hard at him, the vulnerability banished again to be replaced by something much harsher.

'You said you would protect me,' she said. 'The police are supposed to protect vulnerable people.'

'I know.' Harris cast around for the right words. 'And I'm sorry that you feel we have not done so for you. I'll get the lads to keep an eye on you and we'll get forensics to take a look at those stones.'

The sight of the muscular police officer attempting contrition seemed to mollify her. She nodded.

'Thank you,' she said.

It sounded genuine but Harris had already noted how quickly her tone could change, how vulnerability could switch to fury in a matter of seconds. Silence settled on the room, apart from the ticking of the carriage clock. It was Jenny who spoke next.

'I heard the scream again last night, you know,' she said.

Harris stood up. 'I told you, it was probably a vixen.'

'But you're not sure,' she said. 'Are you?'

Deciding not to answer, but disturbed by the way she seemed to always know what he was thinking, the inspector opened the door and walked out into the chill of the morning. Half way across the field, he was met by Gallagher.

'Think we might have an ID,' said the sergeant, glancing down at the notebook in his hand as the two men fell into step down the slope. 'We were right, she's not from round here. From your old neck of the woods, actually.'

'Name?'

'Hannah Matthews. University student in Manchester. Disappeared three days ago. Told her flatmate she had a lecture. The flatmate reported her missing when her bed was not slept in. Turns out there wasn't a lecture either. GMP are emailing us a picture but she's nineteen and blonde.'

'Sounds like our girl,' said Harris bleakly.

'How was the mad woman?'

'Mad.' The inspector glanced along the road and saw a number of curious villagers already making their way towards the scene. 'Make sure uniform keep that lot away, will you? Last thing we want is folks trampling all over our crime scene. You heard from the DI?'

'Yeah. She's setting up an incident room in the conference suite. Oh, and some reporter from local telly has been on to Control. Apparently, someone saw the blues and twos leaving Levton Bridge nick and rang the station.'

'Marvellous,' sighed Harris as they continued walking across the frosty grass. 'Just what we need, TV swanning about like they own the place. I'd better ring the Press Office.'

'Already done. They're sending someone out.'

'Good.' Harris looked at the officers finishing their work on erecting the tent and gave a dark laugh. 'Welcome to the circus, Matty lad.'

Gallagher frowned. Like Harris, he knew the kind of attention that the murder of a young girl attracted from the media. Indeed, on one inquiry during his time in the Met, the sergeant had remonstrated with a television reporter, demanding to know why the murder of a sixty-five-year-old homeless man the previous week had not even warranted a mention on the evening bulletin when the killing of a twenty-two-year-old model just six days later had been the lead story three nights running. 'Just look at her,' the reporter had said without a hint of apology in his voice, 'she's a Bobby Dazzler and the punters love pretty women.' Gallagher had resisted the temptation to slap him but had never forgotten the conversation and it came back to him now as he stood in the field.

'Look after things here, will you?' said Harris. 'Let me know what forensics come up with.'

'Exactly what I hoped you would say,' replied Gallagher ruefully, pulling up his anorak hood as the drizzle started to turn into sleet which drove hard into his face. 'Bit of sun on my back. Although God knows what forensics will turn up in this little lot. You heading back to the factory?'

'Think I'd better,' said the inspector. He looked over at Jenny Meynell's cottage. 'Oh, and keep an eye on her, will you? Maybe pop up and see her at some point?'

Gallagher grimaced. 'Do I have to?'

''Fraid so. Especially if someone holding a television camera knocks on her door.'

The inspector strode over towards his Land Rover, brushing aside questions from the locals who had gathered behind the gate leading out of the field and which was now guarded by one of the uniformed officers. The inspector clambered into his vehicle and, after checking that the dogs were alright in the back, he turned the ignition key and edged the vehicle up alongside the gate, wound down his nearside window and leaned over.

'There really is nothing to see,' he said to the gathered villagers. 'Go home, please.'

He wound the window back but, when they hesitated, wound it down again.

'Go on,' he said, his voice firmer this time. 'I wouldn't want to have to arrest you for obstructing the police. You know I'd do it.'

He gunned the engine. The crowd watched the Land Rover pull away, still uncertain what to do for a moment, torn between dark curiosity about activities in the field and their reluctance to annoy the DCI.

'Best do as he says,' said the uniform sagely. 'You don't want to get on the wrong side of Chief Inspector Harris, do you now?'

After a few more moments, the people turned and started to shuffle back towards the village, exchanging in hushed tones eager speculation about what they had seen. Soon, only Josh Fellows was left at the gate.

'Go on, son,' said the uniformed officer, gesturing towards Carperby. 'On your bike. Nothing to see here.'

'What's happened?' asked Fellows, not moving. 'Is it a dead body? I bet it's a dead body. Is that why they've put that tent up? They do that on the telly news.'

'You heard what the chief inspector said,' replied the uniform. 'Go on, skedaddle, before I nick you.'

'What is it? A man or a woman? Is it a murder? I'll bet it's a murder.'

The officer took a step towards him and Josh Fellows hesitated for a few moments before looking down the road at the retreating Land Rover and holding up his hands in surrender.

'Ok, ok,' he said, starting to walk back towards the village, 'keep your hair on.'

Matty Gallagher had watched the encounter with interest and walked across the field to the gate.

'What'd he want?' asked Gallagher.

'Just a rubbernecker. Josh Fellows. Lives on the green with his mum. That cottage on the end with all the cracked render.'

'Yeah I know it,' nodded Gallagher. 'What do we know about him?'

'Does the gardens over at the old mill the other side of Carperby. You know, the one that's been done up by that businessman.'

'What did he want to know?'

'If we'd found a body and if it was a murder,' said the uniform.

'And that didn't strike you as odd?'

'What, Josh?' The uniformed officer looked at Gallagher in surprise. 'He's harmless, that one. Bit on the simple side, yes, but as harmless as they come. Surely you don't think he had anything to do with this?'

'It's this job,' said Gallagher, watching Josh Fellows until he disappeared round the bend in the road. 'Turns you paranoid.'

'Well, you've got no reason to worry about that one. In fact, you've got nothing to worry about anybody round here.' The officer looked up towards the tent. 'There's no one round here would do something like that.'

Something made Gallagher look across towards Jenny Meynell's cottage. Narrowing his eyes to see better in the half-light, the sergeant could just make her out, standing arms crossed on her doorstep. His attention was distracted by the sound of an engine and he turned to see a white Transit van with faded lettering on the side approaching from the direction of Levton Bridge. The vehicle slowed as the driver peered out curiously at the activity in the field. Waved on by the uniformed officer, the driver accelerated and headed towards the village.

'Who's that?' asked Gallagher.

'Gary Rylance. Runs his own business from Carperby. Delivery driver. He's out all hours, that one.'

'Is he now?'

'You're right,' said the uniform, 'your job does make you paranoid.'

* * *

The Metropolitan Police detective constable stood in the middle of the wasteland and surveyed the burnt-out remains of the vehicle, the twisted and scorched metal making it difficult to recognise as a silver Audi. The partial registration on the number plate, which had somehow survived the blaze, had been the only clue to its identity but even that had turned out to be a dead end. False plates. Narkie Jarvis had not been surprised. Experience told him that the car had most likely been used in a crime, he just did not know what, and with a huge caseload he did not find himself minded to find out unless ordered to do so. His mobile phone rang and he fished it out of his coat pocket.

'DC Jarvis,' he said.

'You after info on a silver Audi?' said a voice.

'Sure am.'

'Well, it seems that it might have come down from the frozen North. ANPR has picked one up coming down from Cumbria way.'

'Who would have thought it,' said Jarvis. He was definitely not going to break into a sweat over it now.

'Hey, didn't your old skipper Matty Gallagher go up there?'

'He did indeed,' said Jarvis. 'No accounting for taste.'

Chapter six

Josh Fellows did go home as instructed by the uniformed police officer at the gate but he was there only briefly. With his mother still sleeping off the previous evening's drinking – the empty cider bottles littered the living room – and the cottage in darkness, he went into the garage to fetch his battered old moped. Relieved that everyone else in the village had gone back into their homes, Josh pushed the bike past the green and onto the main road before starting the engine.

As he did so, he glanced round at the streets leading up the hill to see a white Ford Transit pull up outside one of the terraced houses. Josh recognised the man who got out. Gary Rylance raised an arm in acknowledgement. Josh did not respond and Rylance shrugged and went into his house. It took several attempts for Josh to get his bike started but eventually the aged machine spluttered into life and he donned his crash helmet and rode along the valley road in the opposite direction to the police in the field.

Fifteen minutes later, he was at the mill, standing on the lawn and staring across towards the graves. Eight of them now, their location barely visible through the mist that shrouded the lake. Josh stood there for the best part of twenty minutes, playing the events surrounding the latest girl over and over in his mind. Relishing every sweet moment. Oh, how she had struggled, this one, but he had been too strong for her, he was always too strong for them, and finally she had gone limp. As usual, he did not watch the light dim in her eyes as she became his to dance and dance again.

Josh smiled at the memory but the smile faded when his mind wandered to the way that the uniformed police officer had spoken to him at the gate and he frowned when he recalled the odd look that Gallagher had given him. Did he suspect something? Josh shook his head. What did he know? What did any of them know? He'd got away with all of them without anyone suspecting him. There was no reason to believe that things would be any different now. If they suspected anything, they would have come for him by now and no one had.

Nevertheless, decided Josh as he started walking across the lawn to check that the graves were properly covered up, you could not be too careful. And Sergeant Gallagher would have to be watched carefully. He did not like the way the detective had looked at him. He would have to be dealt with if necessary. Josh wondered what it would be like to throttle the life out a man. He found the idea strangely exciting.

* * *

When Jack Harris arrived at the police station in Levton Bridge, there was already a television company car parked in front of the building. The inspector scowled as he pulled the Land Rover in next to the car, got out and went round to the back of his vehicle to let the dogs out. As he turned to follow them up the steps, the inspector was approached by a young woman clutching a notebook. He recognised her from the local news bulletins and, before she could speak, he shook his head.

'I'm not saying anything at this stage, Avril,' he said, pausing on the third step. 'And I would appreciate it if you didn't pester any of my team. We have an awful lot to do.'

'Yes, but…'

'We'll have a press officer here soon. You can talk to them.'

'We heard that you have sealed off a field near Carperby,' she said as the inspector turned and started walking up the steps again. 'Can you at least tell us what you have found? Is it a body?'

'I'm saying nothing.'

'Come on, Jack. You've got to give us something.'

'I said I'm saying nothing,' snapped the inspector, turning round to glare at her, 'and I've told you before, don't call me Jack. It's Detective Chief Inspector Harris to you.'

'We'll find out anyway.' She glanced at a swarthy man leaning on the car. 'We're on our way over there now to do some filming.'

'Do what you want,' grunted Harris and pushed open the door. 'You'll not get close, though. I've given our lot instructions to kick you off if you make trouble.'

* * *

'Charming,' said the cameraman as the inspector disappeared into the police station.

'Believe me,' said Avril, 'that is charming for Jack Harris. A little bird told me that the Press Office tried to get him to go on some media training a few months ago but he refused point blank. Had to be ordered to go by his commander and walked out after twenty minutes. The trouble with Jack Harris is that he is happy enough to do the media on his own terms, when it's about wildlife, but if someone forces him to do it he gets all bent out of shape.'

'So how come they keep him on?'

'Because everyone you talk to says that he's a bloody good copper.'

'I'd need to be convinced about that,' said the cameraman with a shake of the head as they walked over to their vehicle. 'All I see is a Grade A twat.'

'Just don't say that to his face,' said Avril. 'You wouldn't be the first person he's pinned to the wall.'

'Someone should do something about a bloke like that.'

* * *

When Jack Harris entered the police station, all was well-directed activity. He would have expected nothing else with his detective inspector in charge and, having left the dogs eating their breakfast from the bowls in his office, the DCI walked along the corridor to the incident room to see her. Walking into the room, he noticed Gillian Roberts briefing a small group of detectives over by the window, talking earnestly and occasionally turning to point at the map of the area which she had pinned to the noticeboard. She had already stuck up a post-it note to identify the location of the girl's body. Roberts noticed the DCI at the door, gave some final instructions to the officers and walked over to her boss.

'I don't know,' she said. 'I take a day off and look what happens.'

'Yeah, sorry about that.' Harris looked round the room. 'You seem to have everything under control.'

'Yes, I think so.' A mother-of-two in her early fifties, Gillian Roberts had always said that organising two teenage boys and a husband meant that the rigours of running the day-to-day affairs of CID presented little in the way of challenge. 'I've got a few more coming in. We're going to need all the help we can get on this one. A couple of them gave up rest days.'

'I would expect nothing less. It's always the same with cases like this.'

'She is certainly young,' said Roberts, glancing over to the faxed picture of a laughing Hannah Matthews on a night out, which she had pinned up on the noticeboard, next to the map. 'Just starting out, bless her.'

Harris nodded. He knew that even though her somewhat matronly demeanour masked an officer as tough as they came, the death of someone not much older than her own children would have disturbed the DI.

'Where did we get the picture?' he asked.

'The family gave it to Greater Manchester when she was reported missing.'

'So where are we then?' asked Harris, looking round as two officers carried computers into the room. 'GMP sending someone round to break the bad news to Mum and Dad, I take it?'

'Mum only. Dad died a few years ago. The officers should be with her now.' Roberts gave a shake of the head. 'Poor cow. How do you come to terms with something like that?'

'God knows. There anyone else we need to inform?'

'Hannah had an older sister called Janice. Married with a two-year-old boy. Lives somewhere near Leeds.' She looked again at the picture of a smiling Hannah Matthews. 'Matty seems to think that Hannah might have been kidnapped in Manchester and dumped here?'

'Probably. Did she have a car?'

'Apparently not.'

'Makes abduction more likely then. It certainly wouldn't take the killer that long to get up here from Manchester on quiet roads. I'm just not sure why he chose this area to dump her, though.'

'Could be a local,' said Roberts. 'Picking somewhere he knows?'

'Can't see that.'

'You sure?'

'You're the second person has asked me that this morning. Yeah, I'm sure.'

'Can't rule it out, though.' She eyed him intently. 'Can we?'

'Come on, Gillian, be honest, it doesn't sound like any of ours, does it? Worst we've had over the past few years is a couple of flashers in the park.'

'That's how they start.'

'Yes, I know but it's a hell of a leap from flashing your bits at some woman walking the dog to carrying out a murder. And none of the lads I am thinking of are capable of something like this. I'd stake my pension on it.'

'Unless it's someone beneath the radar.'

Harris frowned. Although he did not admit it, the thought worried him. Worried him when Gallagher queried his boss's certainty back in the field and worried him now, and he found himself reluctantly challenging his beliefs. The inspector's certainty had stemmed from the recognition that the valley was somewhere where everyone knew everyone else's business. It could pose operational difficulties if you wanted to keep something secret but, on the other hand, there was a lot to be said for a place where someone usually saw you wherever you went. The reclusive side to the inspector's personality detested the fact but the policeman in him had been grateful for twitching curtain syndrome on many occasions.

However, even though such a situation meant that crimes committed by local people were usually solved quickly, experience had taught the inspector that, even in the tightest knit communities, it was always possible for some miscreants to slip through the net. Harris stared at the picture of Hannah Matthews on the noticeboard. Had she encountered one such person? Had she inadvertently walked into the dark world of a man whose respectable facade masked a monster? Had he not brought her body here but brought her body *back* here? Had the police, in short, missed something? Had *he* missed something? Harris tried to think if there was something that he had overlooked, a warning sign that he had dismissed as of no consequence at the time. And his mind went back to Jenny Meynell.

Roberts noticed that he had gone quiet.

'What you thinking?' she said.

'About radar. And that we're going to have to get our flashers in for questioning. Do *you* think we might have missed something?'

'Always. However, I'm with you on this one. I can't think of a local who could have done something like this. I'll get someone to track down our flashers anyway.'

The inspector's mobile rang and he fished the device out of his coat pocket and took the call after glancing down at the read-out. It was Leckie.

'Graham,' he said, watching as Roberts took a call of her own and walked over into the corner of the room, deep in conversation. 'They got you in on this one then?'

'All hands to the pump and word is that our local television station already knows about it. You know you'll have a media scrum to deal with, I take it?'

'I've just sent them away with a flea in their ear.'

'The guy that ran that course would be proud of you.'

'He was an idiot, Graham. Look, we're trying to work out if our killer might be one of ours or one of yours. You got anyone at your end?'

'The only ones who might fit the bill are already in clink. We're running some other names.'

'You got anything else on the girl?'

'Bits and bobs. She had just started her second year at Manchester University doing applied mathematics. Bright kid by the sound of it.'

'She from Manchester then?' said Harris, noticing that Roberts had sat down at a nearby desk and was talking earnestly into one of the desk phones while jotting something down.

'Mum and the two kids came to live here after Dad died. Fresh start and all that. Mum was born and bred in the area. She lives in a village just outside the city but Hannah shared a flat with another student in the city. The family used to live in London. Hannah attended primary school there until they moved when she was ten.'

'Funny how London keeps cropping up,' murmured Harris. 'The body turned up near the home of a lunatic called Jenny Meynell. She's just moved up here and keeps hearing a vixen yowling and coming in to report a murder.'

'You tell her what vixens sound like when the urges are upon them?'

'Yeah, but she won't listen.'

'Your questions last night made me suspect that you think you might have a serial killer at work?'

'Actually, I didn't. Only last night, I didn't have a body on my hands.'

'I guess that fishing trip will have to wait.'

'I guess it will.'

As Harris slipped the phone back in his jacket pocket, Roberts ended her call and walked over.

'Did Leckie have anything?' she asked.

'Possibly. It's a hell of a coincidence that the body of a former London primary school pupil was dumped just two hundred metres from the home of a former London primary school teacher, don't you think? I don't believe in coincidences, as well you know, Gillian.'

'Nor me. However, we may have our answer much closer to home. That was Matty Gallagher on the phone. Says that a lad called Josh Fellows was acting suspiciously near where the body was found. Seemed more curious than might seem normal. Asking lots of questions.'

'What, the lad that does the garden at the mill?' Harris shook his head. 'Might be a bit soft in the head but he's no killer.'

'Unless he was under the radar,' said Roberts quietly.

Before he could reply, another of the desk phones rang to be answered by a uniformed officer.

'It's for you, Sir,' she said, holding up the receiver. 'The pathologist. He's out at the field.'

Harris took the call, listened for a few moments, grunted his thanks and handed the receiver back to the girl.

'And?' asked Roberts.

'It's a murder alright. His best guess is that it happened three nights ago. Says the wound could have been caused by some kind of sharp tool. Possibly a garden implement.'

'So now what do you want to do with Josh Fellows?'

'OK,' sighed Harris, 'get Matty to pick him up but tell him to go easy. I don't want him complaining to the chief.'

Chapter seven

The door-to-door teams were on their third street in Carperby when two of them knocked at the terraced house, outside of which stood a white Transit van bearing the words 'G Rylance Ltd – Keeping You Moving', the faded letters only possible to make out against the grimy paintwork by peering closely. The house door was opened by Gary Rylance himself, a tousle-haired man in his thirties, dressed in a dark shirt and smart trousers. He was confronted by a young man in an anorak and a uniformed officer.

'I am sorry to trouble you,' said the man in the anorak, flashing his warrant card. 'I am Detective Constable Alistair Marshall, from Levton Bridge Police Station. This is PC Norris. We are making inquiries about an incident in the area.'

'Is it about what you found in the field?' asked Rylance, letting them into the house and leading them into the living room. 'I noticed you there as I came through. What you found? A body?'

'What makes you say that?'

'The tent. It's like you see on the telly.'

'I can't really say too much at this stage,' said Marshall, accepting the invitation to sit down on the sofa. The uniformed officer remained standing.

'How can I help you anyway?' asked Rylance.

'We are trying to find out if people in the village have seen anything strange over the past two or three days. You know, maybe a vehicle you didn't recognise.'

'I've been away. Sorry,' said Rylance. 'I'm a van driver, run my own business. I have been delivering gear round the Midlands. Only got back an hour or so ago. Look, will this take long? I could really do with some kip.'

Marshall stood up. 'Sure,' he said, heading out into the hall, followed by the uniformed officer. It had been like this at all the houses they had visited so far.

'Hang on a minute,' said Rylance, following him into the hall. 'Come to think of it, there was something. Three nights ago. Tuesday.'

Alistair Marshall looked at him with renewed interest.

'Go on,' he said.

'It was just after 4am. I was away early because I had to be in Coventry for nine. A car went down the main road. A silver Audi, I think it was.'

'You get a registration?'

'Sorry.'

'How many people were in it?'

'I didn't take that much notice,' said Rylance, opening the front door. 'I was loading stuff into the van. Three maybe. It was going at quite a lick.'

'Did you know there was a burglary in a cottage near the village that night?'

'No, but like I said, I've been away.'

'OK,' said Marshall, making a note in his book and stepping into the street. 'Thanks anyway. Mind if I look in your van?'

'Knock yourself out.' Rylance reached up to a hook on the wall and produced a set of keys, which he tossed to the detective.

Marshall unlocked the back doors of the vehicle and peered in. Seeing nothing to alarm him, he locked the doors again and threw the keys back to Rylance, who was standing on the doorstep.

'What you looking for?' asked Rylance.

'Just a routine check. Sorry for the inconvenience.'

'No bother,' replied Rylance and went back into the house, closing the door behind him.

'I take it you didn't see anything?' asked Norris.

'Nah,' said Marshall, rubbing his hands to banish the chill of the morning. 'Come on, let's try next door. Someone's bound to offer us a cuppa soon. I'm bloody freezing.'

* * *

Josh Fellows heard the car approaching down the track to the mill long before he saw the vehicle emerging through the thinning mist. It was shortly after 10.30am and he was engrossed in his work extracting couch grass from one of the flower borders when the rumble of the tyres on gravel caught his attention.

Josh straightened up and watched in silence as a maroon saloon car pulled up outside the cottage and two people got out. One of them was Gallagher, the other a young blonde woman wearing a black coat. Josh had been expecting them but did not speak as the police officers walked across the grass towards him, the man glancing at the molehills scattered around the lawn as he approached.

'You got a bit of a problem there, Josh,' said Gallagher. 'The little buggers are going crackers.'

'Ain't doing no one any harm.'

'That what you think the owner will say when he sees them?' said Gallagher. 'Looks to me like his nice neat and tidy lawn is in a right mess.'

'But you're from away,' replied Josh, before he could think about the wisdom of the comment, 'you would not know about these things.'

'Presumably it's the same thing with the owner,' replied the sergeant, irritated by the comment. 'He's from London, too, I think?'

Josh frowned but said nothing. The sergeant took his warrant card out of his coat pocket.

'Anyway, this isn't Gardener's Question Time,' he said. 'I am from Levton Bridge CID. Detective Sergeant Gallagher. And this is…'

'I know who she is.'

Josh Fellows did indeed know who the blonde woman was. Detective Constable Alison Butterfield. Her parents had owned one of the valley's hill farms for years. Yes, he knew all about Alison Butterfield, had watched her for months, knew everything there was to know about her, where she lived, where she shopped, with whom she socialised. And he had heard people talk about her as well. Feisty, they called her. Outspoken. A real handful, that one, they said. Josh frowned. He did not like girls who fought back.

'So how come you know who I am, Josh?' asked the young detective constable, eying him suspiciously. 'To the best of my knowledge, you and I have never spoken.'

'I've seen you about the place.'

Butterfield continued to eye him dubiously as Matty Gallagher looked round at the grounds, with his gaze eventually straying over to the lake. Josh tried to stay calm under Butterfield's continuing scrutiny.

'You look after all this on your own?' asked Gallagher, returning his attention to the gardener.

'Yeah, just me.'

'A lot of work for one person.'

'I manage.'

'I'm sure you do.' Gallagher's gaze returned to the flower beds, all immaculately tidied up ready for the onset of winter. The sergeant noticed the spade standing up in the soil a few metres away. 'A lot of digging, I should think.'

Josh tried not to look concerned but he could feel himself starting to perspire. Was the detective just making idle conversation or did he know something? Josh felt his hands go clammy and his heart started pounding. He had always known that this moment would come, that they would come for him one day. He had rehearsed his responses time and time again until he knew them off by heart but, now that it was happening, he found himself unnerved by the sergeant's small talk.

'What do you want?' he asked. The question came out much blunter than he had meant and he noticed with alarm the sergeant's irked expression. 'It's just that you can see that I've got a lot to do.'

'It's just a few routine questions,' said Gallagher. 'Nothing to worry about, Josh. Shouldn't take long.'

Josh glanced over to the lake again. The gesture was not lost on the detectives.

* * *

From his position sitting behind a desk at the front of the Levton Bridge Police Station briefing room, Jack Harris surveyed the gathered journalists without much in the way of enthusiasm. Two television crews were setting up their cameras and a couple of radio reporters were preparing to record his comments; there was also a smattering of newspaper reporters, pens at the ready.

Harris had never liked journalists but he had also long realised that, if you wanted to get a message out, the media was the way to do it and, with a case like this, something told him that he would need all the help he could get. Nevertheless, he often found himself repulsed by the journalists' relentless search for the next big story, feelings that stirred again now. There was certainly an excited atmosphere in the room; the journalists had already been briefed by the press officer that the inspector was going to announce the beginning of a major inquiry and there were rumours that the find in the field was the body of a woman. Sensing the anticipation, Jack Harris glanced down at his notes then looked over to the besuited young lady standing in the corner of the room, clutching a notebook. The senior press officer. She looked at the wall clock, just after ten thirty, it said, and she nodded to him. Best get it over with, she thought. No one could see that behind her back she had her fingers crossed. The relationship between Harris and the local media had always been a challenging one. Her hopes of an improvement in his behaviour had risen when his commander persuaded him to attend the media training session a few weeks previously, only to be dashed when he stalked out of the room after twenty minutes.

'Thank you for attending this press conference,' said Harris, trying to sound polite. 'I know that you have been very patient and I thank you for that. I apologise for not being able to give you much information before now.'

'Or *any* information,' said a man's voice from the floor but the inspector could not see who had spoken.

The press officer held her breath.

'Yes, well,' continued Harris, trying to control his irritation and conscious that the cameras were now rolling, 'be that as it may…'

'We heard that you found the body of a girl, Chief Inspector. Is that true?' asked one of the newspaper reporters.

'Yes. The body of a nineteen-year-old girl who went missing from Manchester earlier this week was found in a field near Carperby just under four hours ago. We are treating her death as suspicious.'

A murmur rippled round the room. Some of the journalists glanced at the wall clock, calculating how much time they had until the next deadline.

'I can also tell you the girl's identity,' said the inspector, glancing down at a piece of paper on the desk. He did not need to, though; he knew that the girl's name would be seared into his brain until he went to his grave. 'Hannah Matthews. She lived in the Manchester area, attended university in the city and was last seen on Tuesday. We think that she probably died that evening.'

'How did she die?' asked Avril.

'From a head injury. However, until the pathologist has completed his examination I cannot be more specific than that.'

There was a brief silence in the room then the inspector remembered what the press officer had told him in the moments before the conference began. A sound bite, she had said, give them a soundbite. Keep them happy.

'What I can say, though,' he said, his mind going back to Hannah's lifeless eyes and finding himself speaking with genuine feeling, 'that whoever did this is extremely dangerous and that everyone involved in this inquiry is determined to bring him to justice for the sake of this poor girl and her family.'

The reporters scribbled furiously and the press officer gave the inspector a nod of approval.

* * *

'I saw you back there at the field,' said Gallagher, noticing that beads of sweat had started on Josh Fellows's brow, glistening in the chill of the morning. 'You seemed to be very interested in what was happening.'

'Wouldn't you be interested? Lots of police officers turning up not far from your home. You'd be interested in that, I reckon.'

'I guess I would, Josh.'

'Mind, I'm not that interested,' said Josh, unnerved by the way that the sergeant did not follow up the comment with anything else. Butterfield took her lead from Gallagher and said nothing. 'I mean, it ain't nothing to do with me.'

'Course it isn't,' said the sergeant.

There was more silence for a few moments broken only by the raucous cawing of a crow in the nearby copse and, when the detective sergeant noticed that Butterfield appeared about to speak, he gave the slightest shake of the head so the constable kept her thoughts to herself. Matty Gallagher knew that silence was a powerful tool when it came to nervous suspects.

'So, is it a body?' asked Josh after a few seconds, allowing curiosity to get the better of him. 'I mean, in the field, is it a body that you found?'

There you go, thought Gallagher, noticing that more beads of sweat were glistening on the gardener's brow. A few more moment's silence.

'What do you think?' asked Gallagher eventually, eying him intently. 'Do you think it's a body in the field, Josh?'

Joss shrugged. 'How would I know?' he said.

'Indeed,' murmured Gallagher. 'And as it goes, you're right, it was the body of a girl. Where were you three nights ago?'

The question seemed to take Josh off guard. Again he glanced over towards the lake. Again the detectives noticed the gesture.

'Why do you want to know where I was?' asked Josh.

'It's just a routine question,' said the sergeant.

'At home.' Josh nodded his head to confirm the fact. 'Finished off here when it got dark then went straight back for my tea.'

'And then?'

'Stayed in all night. Watching TV.'

'What did you watch?' asked Gallagher.

'Midsomer Murders.' Josh did not appear to notice the irony in his reply.

'And what happened in Midsomer Murders?' asked the sergeant.

'Some bloke got his head stoved in with a pitchfork.'

Gallagher nodded. He had watched the same programme after Julie had set off for her night shift, the sergeant sitting on the sofa working his way through a four-pack of lager.

'Anyone confirm that you were at home, Josh?' asked Butterfield. 'I mean, just because you know what was on the programme does not prove that you are telling the truth.'

'My mother,' said Josh, his mind going back to the cider bottles still scattered round the living room. He seemed to the detectives to be more confident now. 'Yes, she were in all night. She's in every night these days. She'll tell you that I did not go out again. Stayed in and watched the telly, like I said.'

'Then you've got nothing to worry about, have you?' said Gallagher. He gave a reassuring smile then looked at the garden. 'Mind if we have a look round?'

'Why?'

'Call it idle curiosity, Josh,' said Gallagher. 'I might pick up some tips about growing daffodils.'

'They don't come out until the spring.'

'OK if we have a wander anyway?'

Josh looked uneasy but nodded and watched in silence as the detectives strolled across the lawn before taking the path which wound its way through the trees and emerged on the edge of the lake. The officers stared out across to the hills, the only sound the lapping of the water against the nearby wooden jetty.

'So, what do you think?' asked Butterfield. She glanced back through the trees to where Josh was still standing watching them. 'He kept looking over here.'

'Yeah, I noticed that.'

'And he's nervous as hell. Very edgy.'

'Granted, but we can have that effect on people. Particularly those who may not be all there. And I'd be curious if a load of plod turned up next to my home and started putting up a tent.'

'But he could still be our man.' Her eyes gleamed. 'I mean, he's acting very suspiciously. Maybe we could have found our killer, Sarge. Wow, what would the DCI say if we went back having…?'

'Did you notice the crappy old moped?' asked Gallagher.

'What moped?' She looked back through the trees towards the house and saw for the first time the mud-spattered bike leaning against the coal shed. 'Yeah, what of it?'

'Can't see him getting a body on the back of that and driving it up the M6 without anyone noticing,' said Gallagher. 'Can you? In fact, I'm amazed that it got him from Carperby.'

Cursing inwardly at overseeing the vehicle at a time when she was trying to prove herself worthy of the switch from uniform to CID, Butterfield shook her head.

'No,' she said glumly. 'No, I can't.'

'Observation, Constable,' said the sergeant. 'It's the first rule of what we do.'

'I know but what if Hannah got herself here then?'

Gallagher did not reply. The thought had been nagging away at him all morning and he found himself irritated that it had taken a rookie to remind him of the fact. Gallagher turned towards the house and saw Josh Fellows staring at him. *Through* him. For a moment, just the briefest of moments, the sergeant felt his blood run cold. The sensation only lasted a fraction of a second, though, then it was gone.

'Come on,' said Gallagher. 'Let's get out of here.'

'Don't you want to take him in for questioning?'

'No.'

'But what if…?'

'For fuck's sake! Will you stop challenging what everyone says! I've warned you about this before.'

Butterfield looked crestfallen.

'I'm sorry,' said the sergeant quickly, noting her expression. His tone softened. 'Shouldn't have shouted. The DCI said to take it easy with the kid unless we had something concrete to go on and I've not seen anything. Have you?'

Butterfield shook her head.

'No,' she said glumly, 'no, I haven't.'

'Come on,' said Gallagher, patting her on the arm and starting to walk again. 'Let's get back to the field. Last I heard, Alfie Myles was going to rustle up some tea and I'm bloody freezing.'

* * *

'Do you have anyone in custody, Chief Inspector?' asked one of the newspaper reporters.

'No, not yet.'

'Do you…?'

'Look,' said the inspector, interrupting the reporter, 'this inquiry really is in its very early stages and there is an awful lot of work to do, so it is far too early to be talking about arrests. We will, of course, be working very closely with our colleagues at Greater Manchester Police.'

'So does that mean that you think the killer is most likely to come from Manchester?' asked another reporter.

'Like I say, it is far too early to speculate. We will be talking to a number of people of interest at this end as well.'

'So the killer could come from the Levton Bridge area?'

'I am not prepared to say,' replied Harris, trying to conceal his irritation at what he saw as a repeat of the same question.

'But you cannot rule it out?' asked the reporter.

Harris thought for a few moments and noticed that all the journalists were eying him intently. The press officer held her breath.

'I cannot rule anything out at this stage,' said Harris eventually, 'but I can say that I would be very surprised if the killer did turn out to be from here. Very surprised indeed.'

* * *

'He may be an oddball,' said Gallagher as he and Butterfield walked along the mill house drive towards the car, 'but he's not a killer. I'm pretty sure about that.'

'There's something still not right about him, though.'

'If we locked up everyone who was not right, the cells would be overflowing.'

They reached the car and Gallagher scraped the mud off his shoes on one of the tyres then fished in his trouser pocket for his keys.

'Mr Gallagher.'

The sergeant turned to see Josh Fellows approaching slowly across the lawn towards them. He was trembling slightly and the colour had drained from his cheeks.

'Josh,' said Gallagher, walking towards him, followed by Butterfield, 'are you alright?'

The gardener did not reply but came to a halt on the edge of the grass and stood staring blankly at them.

'Is there something you want to tell me?' asked the sergeant, alarmed by the distant expression on his face.

'That girl. The one the radio said you found in the field?'

'What about her?'

'I killed her,' said Josh. 'Would you like me to show me where I buried the body?'

The detectives stared at him in bewilderment.

'Buried her?' said Gallagher. 'Buried who?'

'The girl.' Josh seemed exasperated at the detectives' slow reactions to what he was saying. 'She's with the other ones now.'

'Other ones?' said Gallagher, still looking bewildered. 'What do you mean, the other ones, Josh?'

Josh turned and gestured to the lake.

'There's eight of them now. I dug graves round the edge of the lake.' Josh gave a half smile. 'Are you going to arrest me?'

Standing there on that gravel path on a cold autumn morning and looking at the young man holding out his hands to be cuffed, Matty Gallagher fancied that he could hear the faint sound of music over the northern hills. Then it was gone.

Chapter eight

The press conference over, a relieved Jack Harris had a quick chat with the press officer then strode from the room, curtly rebuffing requests from the media for further interviews. Half way down the corridor, he was called back by a woman's voice. He turned to see Avril and the cameraman walking towards him.

'Can I have a word?' asked the television reporter. She glanced behind her and noticed that other reporters had also left the briefing room and were eying the conversation with interest. 'In private?'

'I told you back there, Avril,' said Harris. 'I am not doing any interviews.'

'Yes, but…'

'Which bit of "no interviews" are you struggling with?' snapped Harris. 'It's not that difficult, surely? Even for a television reporter.'

'Hey,' protested the cameraman, 'she's only doing her job, pal. She doesn't deserve that.'

Harris glowered at him – no one called him pal and he'd dropped men for less. Working hard to control his temper, the inspector turned to start walking along the corridor again.

'We'll just have to interview her without checking with you then,' said Avril. 'Seems like she might have quite a story to tell, thought you might like to give a comment.'

'Who?' asked Harris, turning back to her and not wanting to hear the reply. 'Interview who?'

'Like you don't know?' Avril glanced down at her notebook. 'She's called Jenny Meynell.'

'What has she been saying?' asked Harris sharply.

'Can we go somewhere else, please?' Avril looked back at the other reporters. 'Don't want them nicking our exclusive.'

'She's hardly an exclusive.' Seeing the determined look on her face, Harris sighed and led them into an empty office, closing the door once they were in. He sensed that the time had come for some charm so he tried to sound polite.

'Look, Avril, I would rather that you did not talk to Jenny Meynell,' he said. 'That really would not be particularly helpful at this stage in the investigation.'

'You'll have to do better than that, Chief Inspector. The word is that she has been warning you about a possible murder and you ignored her, which would be a good enough story but coming so soon after the chief constable's memo…' She did not finish the sentence, she did not need to.

Harris tried another tack, scowled and attempted to imbue his voice with a sense of menace.

'Look, Avril,' he growled, taking a step closer to her, noticing that the cameraman had bunched his right fist, 'I am telling you for your own good not to talk to Jenny Meynell.'

'For my own good?' said Avril. 'Is that a threat, Chief Inspector?'

'No, of course not,' said Harris quickly, sensing that he had met his match in the feisty young reporter. 'I am just trying to tell you that if you run something on Jenny Meynell, you will end up looking pretty stupid.'

'Really? From what we have been told, she told you that she heard screams. Thought it was a woman being murdered.'

'Yes, well, it wasn't. If you ask me, it was a vixen.'

'Are you sure about that? I mean, you *have* got a dead woman on your hands, have you not?'

Harris looked hard at her then, overcome by a sudden and overwhelming irritation at people continually questioning his judgement, he opened the door and stalked from the office.

'Just keep the fuck away from her,' he said over his shoulder. 'The press officer will see you out.'

'Jesus,' said the shaken cameraman when the detective had gone, 'I thought he was going to deck me.'

The press officer walked into the office. She looked worried.

'What did you say to Jack?' she asked. 'He looks furious.'

'We wanted to know if it would be ok to interview Jenny Meynell.'

The press officer looked even more worried.

'We'd rather you didn't, you know,' she said.

'I bet you would,' said Avril.

Still fuming at the encounter with the television crew, the inspector strode along the corridor and into the incident room where he headed for Gillian Roberts, who was standing by the map, pointing something out to a uniformed officer.

'I take it things didn't go well then?' she said, breaking off her conversation when she saw the DCI's thunderous expression.

'The press conference went ok, don't think I said anything too stupid, but Avril whatsername asked me about Jenny Meynell afterwards.'

'And you said?'

'I requested that they steer clear of her.'

Roberts raised an eyebrow. 'Requested?' she said.

'OK,' sighed Harris, 'maybe requested is not quite the right word.'

Roberts was about to reply when the nearest desk phone rang. She picked it up and listened for a few moments then replaced the receiver.

'The day might just have taken a turn for the better,' she said. 'Looks like we've got an arrest.'

'I assume that was Manchester on the blower then?' Harris clapped his hands together. 'Boy, they moved fast.'

'Actually, it was Matty. Looks like our killer may have been much closer to home. A local.'

'A local?' said Harris in a hollow voice. 'Not the daft lad who works at the mill?'

'Confessed the lot. Reckons he's killed eight of them.'

'Eight?' said the perplexed inspector. 'We haven't got eight missing women.'

'Matty admits that some of the things he's saying don't add up but the lad is adamant that he did it. He told them that there's bodies buried in the grounds. Forensics are on their way over there now, see what they can find.'

Harris cast his mind back to the press conference and closed his eyes.

'What was that about not saying anything stupid?' he groaned. 'They'll definitely have me on that bloody training course now.'

* * *

Jenny Meynell was dozing on the sofa when a loud knock at the door to the cottage startled her out of slumber. After a few moments to gather her thoughts, she walked into the hallway and tentatively opened the door; very few people visited the cottage and she had been warned about letting strangers in. Standing outside were a young woman and a man.

'Jenny Meynell?' asked the woman. 'My name is Avril Hardy from Look North West. I take it you know that a body has been found in the field?'

Jenny nodded.

'We wondered if we could interview you about the screams you heard?' continued Avril. 'It sounds like you could have some very important information.'

'Would I have to appear on camera?'

'Ideally, yes.' Avril glanced at her partner. 'Dave is the cameraman.'

'No, I don't think so. Not on camera.'

'What if you did not have to appear on camera?' asked Avril. 'Just tell us the story. From what we hear the police treated you very badly. DCI Jack Harris, wasn't it?'

'I am not sure that…'

'Do you not want people to know what happened? I mean, they had that memo from the chief constable yet here they were dismissing your reports. You are a respectable citizen just trying to help.'

'They wouldn't take me seriously, it's true. It was very hurtful, the way they behaved. DCI Harris was very dismissive of what I was trying to tell him. They all were.'

'So I hear. Perhaps we can come in and talk about the police shortcomings? Over a nice cup of tea, maybe?'

'I am not sure that would be allowed.'

'Allowed? This is not a police state, Jenny. DCI Harris cannot tell people what to say.'

'I was not thinking of DCI Harris.'

'Then who…?'

'No,' said Jenny, making her mind up and closing the door in their faces.

Avril was about to knock again when she heard the sound of tyres and turned to see a police patrol vehicle edging its way up the muddy path leading to the cottage. When it came to a halt, two stern-faced uniformed officers got out and walked purposefully towards the television crew. She held her hands up in mock surrender.

'Ok, ok, we're going,' she said.

As they got into their car and Dave started the engine, Avril's mobile phone rang. She listened for a few moments then ended the call and looked across to the cameraman, her eyes gleaming.

'You and me will be on the national news, I reckon,' she said. 'This story just keeps getting better and better. Looks like we've got a serial killer on our hands.'

'Bingo,' said the cameraman.

Chapter nine

'I've called in the divers as well,' said Gallagher as he and Harris stood in front of the mill that lunchtime and watched a team of police officers digging up the grassy area round the lake.

'Are you sure about all this?' asked the inspector.

'Not really.' Gallagher noticed the inspector's dubious expression. 'But we have to look, don't we? I mean, the lad *has* coughed to eight murders and says he buried the bodies here.'

'I guess so but it does rather ignore the fact that one of the bodies he claims to have buried is currently lying in the morgue at Roxham General Hospital. She can't be in two places at once, can she?'

'I know, I know,' sighed Gallagher.

The detectives stood in gloomy silence for a few moments, watching a couple of officers pushing their way carefully through the bedraggled patches of reeds fringing the edge of the lake, searching for any sign that would lead them to graves. The inspector tried to push scepticism to the corner of his mind and look at it from his sergeant's point of view. And when he did that, he had to admit that if you *were* going to bury bodies anywhere, this would make an excellent place. Remote location, few visitors and the graves dug by the only person who worked the garden. Yes, thought Harris, it would make a good place to bury your victims. And yet, and yet, and yet…

'So *are* they really out there?' asked Harris, glancing at his sergeant. 'Are we dismissing the idea of these murders too easily, Matty lad?'

'We?'

'OK,' said Harris, 'am *I* dismissing it too lightly? *Are* we looking at a graveyard? A serial killer that we knew nothing about?'

'Jenny Meynell would love that,' said Gallagher. 'But, no, I reckon we're just going through the motions. If you ask me, he's a bit soft in the head is our Josh. Making it all up. It could well turn into a nuthouse job.'

Harris nodded and turned at the sound of shoes on gravel as the press officer walked towards them.

'Sorry, Jack,' she said, 'but there's a load of media just turned up at the front gate.'

'How did they find out we were here?'

'One of the newspaper lads said his newsdesk got a tip-off. They want to know what we're doing here.'

'Couldn't you fob them off?'

'I tried to, and uniform had to stop Sky filming over the fence, but they insist on talking to you.'

'I'll bet they do,' said Harris. 'Must be my sparkling personality.'

The press officer looked doubtful, an expression that brought forth a low laugh from Gallagher.

'Yeah, that'll be it, guv,' said the sergeant. 'Your sparkling personality.'

Harris gave a rueful look, glanced at the hills and sighed. How he wished he was up there now, him and the dogs making their way across the moorland, well away from the circus that always surrounded murder inquiries like this. Harris noted that, with the drizzle starting to fall harder now, mists had started to gather on the tops of the hills. Experience told him that it would not be long until they vanished from view. The inspector noticed the press officer looking expectantly at him.

'Yeah, ok, Georgia,' he sighed. 'I'll talk to them.'

'Thanks, Jack, I know you don't like them.'

'Whatever gave you that idea?' said Harris, walking back towards the house. 'I love journos, me.'

Gallagher watched him trudge down the drive in the direction of the front gate, followed by the forlorn figure of the press officer.

'Good luck,' shouted Gallagher.

'Thanks, I'll need it,' said Harris without turning round.

'I was thinking of Georgia,' grinned Gallagher.

Harris flapped a hand and kept walking. As they disappeared round the corner of the house, the sergeant's mobile phone rang. He sighed. It had been ringing all morning. 'Gallagher,' he said, taking the call. The readout told him it was from Lorna in Traffic.

'Sorry it's taken so long to get back to you,' she said. 'We got roped in on that big drugs job down near Carlisle. Anyway, that silver Audi you were looking for after the old couple's house got screwed the other night? Well, we may have something for you.'

'Go on.' Gallagher realised that the murder had driven all thought of the incident from his mind. He recalled the crowd outside the surgery. Remembered Jim Garbutt's grey face as he was loaded into the ambulance. 'I really need to show that we're doing something. The natives are distinctly restless.'

'Hope this helps then. Turns out it was spotted the night before the break-in, mooching round a village near Roxham.'

'Alistair Marshall found someone who saw it up here as well. Your witness get a number?'

'Matched a car in Redbridge. You know it?'

84

'Yeah, used to play five-a-side with the lads from the local nick. You got an address then?'

'Ah, that's where I stop being helpful, I am afraid. The local cops talked to the owner, a broker in the City, and he swears blind it's been sitting in a local garage with a busted catalytic converter for four days. What's more, his car is a 4x4.'

'Fake plates then.'

'Looks like it. ANPR clocked it several times in the hours after your old couple were done over. Heading south on the M6. CCTV spotted it dropping a guy off at a motorway services near Liverpool. Fuzzy image, not enough to give an ID. Then it headed on down to Redbridge where the Met found it dumped and set on fire. That's all I've got, I am afraid. Tell Julie I'll ring her in a day or two to sort a girly night out.'

'Will do.'

Gallagher slipped the phone back into his coat pocket and stared out over the garden. The rain had started to fall much harder now and the clouds had obscured the summits of the hills. A uniformed officer walked across the lawn towards Gallagher, clutching a spade and with mud spattering his face.

'We could look very stupid here,' he said. 'Very stupid indeed.'

'Although not as stupid as you look. You seem to have brought half the garden with you.'

'It's filthy down there,' said the uniform, wiping some of the specks off with a grubby handkerchief. 'You CID boys ought to try getting your hands dirty. You sure about this?'

'Funny, you're about the millionth person to have asked me that this morning. Apparently, the chief has been onto Curtis to express his full confidence in me. Oh, no, hang on, that's not what he said.'

'You can't blame him, can you?'

'Thanks for your support,' grunted Gallagher. 'Means such a lot to me at a time like this.'

'I've known Josh Fellows since he was knee high to a grasshopper,' said the uniform. 'He may be a bit slow on the uptake but I'd bet my pension that the lad's not a murderer.'

'Yeah, but we have to make sure.'

'You keep saying it – eventually someone will believe you.'

Before the detective sergeant could reply, his mobile phone rang again.

'This had better be good news,' he grunted as he took the call. 'Ah, Constable Butterfield, please enrich my day and confirm that meladdo went AWOL for a spot of butchery three nights ago.'

'Sorry, Sarge,' said Butterfield. 'Took me ages to rouse Mum. She'd clearly been at it all night, there were empty bottles all over the floor.'

'And what did she say, as if I didn't know?'

'That Josh was telling the truth about Tuesday. Came back from work just before five and did not go out again. Watched telly. She swears blind it's true.'

'More like blind drunk,' sighed Gallagher, ending the call and turning to look once more at the officers digging down by the lake. 'Something tells me that this day is going from bad to worse.'

He dialled a number.

'Alistair? You still in Carperby? Good, can you check something out for me?'

* * *

Alistair Marshall knocked on the door to the terraced house, which was opened by Gary Rylance, now dressed in blue shorts and a black Alice Cooper T-shirt adorned with a screaming skull. He had a toothbrush in his hand.

'Hello again,' said the van driver, looking at the detective and his uniformed colleague. 'I was just about to go to bed.'

He gestured for them to enter but Marshall shook his head.

'This won't take a moment,' said Marshall. 'The car you told us about earlier? The silver Audi. Any chance it might have been a 4x4?'

Rylance shook his head.

'No, definitely an Audi,' he said. 'My brother had one.'

Marshall nodded his appreciation.

'Thanks anyway,' he said. 'Have a good sleep.'

* * *

The sister on Ward 43 at Hafton General Hospital had only just slipped off her shoes and sat down with a cup of tea and the latest edition of Women's Own at the nurse's station when the alarm went off. With a sigh, she let the magazine slide to the floor and placed the cup on the desk – another one to go cold, she thought gloomily – and, after a regretful glance at her still unwrapped sandwich, she walked briskly down the corridor to one of the side rooms, reaching the door just as one of the nurses got there.

The women walked into the room and surveyed the old man in the bed. Jim Garbutt's breathing was shallow and the colour had drained from his face. Death was close. The young nurse moved towards the bed as the old man started to emit a low croaking sound but the sister tapped her softly on the arm.

'Let him go, Julie,' she said quietly.

'But maybe we can…'

'If it's not today, it will be tomorrow, love.' The sister smiled sadly. 'There really is nothing more that we can do for him.'

Julie looked at the old man.

'If you're sure,' she said.

'Much better to just let him go. And when he has, you'd better ring that boyfriend of yours. He'll want to know, I am sure.' The sister glanced up at the wall clock.

'And then go home. You were supposed to have knocked off two hours ago.'

* * *

After the television crew had left, Jenny Meynell stood at her living room window for the best part of thirty minutes and watched the officers as they painstakingly worked their way across the field, down on their hands and knees, fingers feeling for anything that might lead them to the killer. It was clear to Jenny that they had found nothing and, when she tired of the spectacle, she turned back into the room and walked into the kitchen, where she busied herself making a cup of tea.

Having switched on the kettle, she glanced up at the wall clock and reached across the worktop to switch on her radio, frowning as she heard the familiar hiss through which could just be discerned the crackle of a distant echoing voice. Jenny sighed – one of the things that she found hardest to come to terms with since her move north was the poor radio reception in the valley. An avid Radio 4 listener when she lived in London, she had missed being able to tune into her favourite programmes and had instead been forced to resort to the local station. Jenny did not like listening to it – she had always turned her nose up at commercial radio – but it was noise and Jenny Meynell had found herself appreciating the company in her lonely cottage on the hill.

Suddenly, as was the radio's want, there was a burst of clarity and she heard the sound of the news jingle, blaring out. She reached over to adjust the volume.

'This is the news at one o'clock,' said a man's voice. 'Our top story: police investigating the murder of a young woman found in a field outside the village of Carperby this morning have now named her.'

Jenny paused with the box of teabags in her hand and craned closer to the radio as the hiss started up again, making the words difficult to decipher.

'Detective Chief Inspector Jack Harris, the officer leading the investigation, said that the dead woman was Hannah Matthews, aged nineteen, from the Manchester area.'

Jenny stared at the radio.

'According to DCI Harris,' continued the news reader, 'the Manchester University student disappeared having told her flatmate that she was going to attend a lecture that did not exist. It is understood that Hannah originally hails from London before moving north with her mother and sister ten years ago. Here's our reporter Gavin Hallett with the story…'

But Jenny Meynell was not listening. The blood drained from her face and she sat down heavily on a chair and stared in disbelief at the radio as the crackling drowned out the reporter's words.

'Dear God, no,' she murmured.

Chapter ten

Jack Harris stared bleakly at the journalists gathered
expectantly at the front gate of the mill house, huddled
under the trees as the rain started to fall. Their demeanour
suggested that they were not in the mood to be fobbed off
by an irritable detective chief inspector feeling the effects
of his disturbed night. This was a big story and getting
bigger all the time and their newsdesks were pushing hard
for the latest angle.

The inspector glanced at the press officer who tried
not to let her concern show. Bitter experience had taught
her that Harris did not respond well when pushed for
answers by journalists. She knew that he was still irked by
events at a press conference held at Levton Bridge Police
Station several weeks previously, which was supposed to
discuss a new anti-burglary initiative but which turned into
a series of questions about the chief constable's memo
after it was leaked to the local television station. After
several minutes, the DCI had brought proceedings to an
end and stalked angrily from the room, subsequently
berating the press officer as if she were responsible for
what had happened.

As Georgia walked over to brief the journalists, Avril Hardy broke away from the group and walked over to the inspector.

'Don't think you can shut everyone up,' she said to the detective.

'What?'

'Telling Jenny Meynell she was not allowed to talk to us. That's a cheap trick. She can talk to who she wants to. I have half a mind to submit a formal complaint about you.'

Harris looked bewildered. 'I didn't tell her anything of the sort,' he said.

'Of course you didn't,' said Avril and walked back to listen to the press officer's briefing, watched in bemusement by the inspector. A few moments later, Georgia glanced back at Harris.

'Ready?' she said.

'Yeah, sure.' He took a step forward and surveyed the journalists. 'So what would you like to know?'

'Can you confirm that you are digging up the garden?' asked one of the newspaper reporters.

'I imagine that you have already seen that for yourselves.' Harris glanced at the Sky Television news cameraman. 'Some closer than others. Although I would remind you that it is private property and any attempt to get in will be deemed to be trespass. But yes, I can confirm that we are conducting a search of the gardens.'

'Can you tell us why?'

'Routine inquiries.'

'It's hardly routine if you've got police officers digging holes all over the place,' said another reporter.

'Routine inquiries,' insisted the inspector.

'Come on, Chief Inspector,' said the reporter. 'At least give us something. You know that our newsdesks will keep pushing us until you do.'

The press officer held her breath.

'Ok, ok,' said Harris. 'I can confirm that we are searching the garden following information received from a member of the public in connection with an ongoing inquiry.'

'Into the death of Hannah Matthews?'

Harris nodded. 'Yes.'

'What are you looking for?'

'I am not at liberty to divulge that at this stage.'

'Are you looking for more bodies?' asked one of the newspaper reporters. 'Do you think that you have a serial killer operating in the area, Chief Inspector? Are there more victims?'

'Like I said, Terry, I really am not in a position to comment further until we have something more definite.'

'Digging lots of holes seems very definite to me.'

'Look,' and Harris gave them all a stern look, 'talk of a serial killer at this stage is not at all helpful. There is absolutely nothing to suggest that we have more than one murder and I would appreciate it if you avoided fuelling speculation when you come to make your reports. The last thing we want to do is to frighten…'

'Is it true that you have arrested someone?' asked Avril, cutting across him. 'That's what we have heard anyway. That you have a young man in custody.'

Harris frowned at the interruption.

'We have taken a man into custody, yes,' he said, picking his words carefully and wondering where she was getting her information.

'From this area?'

'Yes.'

'But you said you didn't think that was possible. You said that you would be very surprised if that turned out to be the case.'

Before the inspector could reply, a shout went up from the garden and the journalists craned their necks to see past him. Gratefully, Harris grunted his apologies and began to walk briskly back down the drive. The excited journalists tried to follow him but found their way barred by two uniformed officers.

Leaving the sound of their remonstrations behind him, the inspector strode down the drive in the direction of the lakeside where a number of officers were clustered round one of the holes that they had just excavated. His relief at being rescued from the journalists' relentless questioning was quickly overtaken by a sense of foreboding as he cut across the lawn. The inspector had already decided that Josh Fellows was making up stories but the thought that the officers might have actually found a body sent a chill down his spine. He had always worried that working in an area where everyone knew everyone's business could breed complacency that might blunt a police officer's instincts. Even those of an experienced detective such as him. The thought struck him forcibly now. It also struck the press officer as she struggled to keep up with the inspector's loping strides across the grass.

'Perhaps we *do* have a serial killer,' she said, catching up with him.

'I bloody hope not,' grunted Harris. 'Whole new ball game that is.'

'It certainly is,' nodded the press officer as they approached the lake. 'We'll get the international media then. What we've had so far is nothing as to the way they behave.'

'Oh, joy,' said Harris as he stepped onto the muddy path winding its way through the trees.

The uniformed officers standing at the edge of the lake moved aside to let the inspector through to where a grim-faced Matty Gallagher was staring down at a collection of bones gathered in the bottom of the hole.

'It would appear,' said Gallagher in a flat voice as the inspector came to stand next to him, 'that young Josh might have been telling the truth.'

'Not so sure about that,' said Harris, crouching down. 'They don't look human to me.'

'I hope you're right,' said Gallagher.

'So do I.'

* * *

Josh Fellows sat in the cramped little cell at Levton Bridge Police Station and stared at the blank walls. His heart was pounding, his hands were clammy and his head hurt. The door opened and a uniformed officer walked in.

'You alright, son?' he said. 'You look very pale.'

'I don't feel very well. Dizzy.'

'Want me to get the doctor?'

'Please,' he said, adding as the officer turned to go, 'When will I get to see Sergeant Gallagher? I want to see Sergeant Gallagher.'

'I am afraid that he is still out.' Something in the young man's voice alerted the officer's interest. 'Why, is there something you want to tell him?'

Josh shook his head and closed his eyes.

'No, he'll find out soon enough,' he said.

'Find out what?'

'Nothing.'

The uniformed officer sat down next to him.

'Look,' he said, 'if there's something you want to tell the sergeant, he can be here in twenty minutes. Don't make sense to keep it all bottled up.'

'I'll talk to him when he's finished what he's doing.'

'Digging up your garden, that's what he's doing.'

Josh said nothing.

'Have it your way,' replied the officer and stood up. 'I'll get the doctor for you.'

And the door clanged to leave Josh Fellows alone with his demons dancing a dance of their own.

* * *

The pathologist, a crusty character in his mid-sixties who smelled of old tweed and damp towels, stood next to Gallagher and Harris and stared down at the bones. His knees cracked as he crouched to afford himself a better view and he winced at the pain. So did the others. After thinking for a few more moments and running his fingers through the soil, the pathologist shook his hands to get rid of the mud, gave a satisfied grunt and accepted Harris's assistance in straightening up, rubbing his knee once he had done so.

'Well?' asked Gallagher. 'We got ourselves a murder victim, doc?'

'No, you have not. Your governor is right – these bones aren't human.'

'What are they then? Animal?'

'He's sharp this one,' said the pathologist, winking at Harris, who smiled. 'Best guess? I'd say what you have got here is a Labrador, or a Golden Retriever maybe, something like that. And I reckon it's been there a while.'

'Yeah, I'll go with that,' said the inspector. He turned to look back at the house. 'An old family pet, maybe. Any idea how it died?'

'I'm a pathologist, not a vet, Jack.'

'Fair enough,' said the inspector.

His mobile phone rang.

'Hawk?' said Gillian Robert's voice as the inspector took the call. 'You ok to talk?'

'Yeah, no problem,' said Harris, walking away to stand on his own underneath the trees. 'It's like bloody Crufts here. What you got for me? How's Mum?'

'In bits. I've booked her into a local b. & b., said that you'd talk to her when you got back. I've got a WPC sitting with her and the sister, but that's not why I rang. Jenny Meynell has just been into reception, demanding to see you. Won't talk to anyone else. Says it's important. Something about Hannah Matthews' death.'

'I don't have time for her at the moment,' said Harris. 'I know she's scared but if the media keep whipping this serial killer thing up, everyone will be scared.'

'Especially if the dead girl found near your home used to be in your class.'

'What?'

'I finally managed to persuade her to confide in me. Took her to the canteen for a cup of coffee. You know

Leckie said that before Hannah Matthews and her family came north, she was a pupil at the school in London? Well, according to Jenny, she taught Hannah for two years. She was one of her favourite pupils.'

Harris stared across to the hills but said nothing. Sometimes, he thought, life up on the tops, just him and the dogs, was so much more simple.

'Are we sure about this?' he asked.

'I've got someone checking with the school but Jenny seemed pretty sure that it was the same girl. If it is true, it's one hell of a coincidence – and we all know Jack Harris's first law of investigations, don't we?'

'Don't believe in coincidences,' murmured the inspector.

'Exactly.'

Five minutes later, the journalists at the front gate parted to let the chief inspector's Land Rover pass and head at speed in the direction of Levton Bridge. Back on the lakeside, as Gallagher stood and watched the vehicle wind out of view, his mobile rang yet again. This time it was Julie. He took the call.

'Hi, love,' he said. 'Thought you'd be getting some kip by now.'

'I had to stay on a bit. I'm off in a couple of minutes, though.'

'At least you won't be ringing to give me bad news.'

'You wish,' said Julie. 'I am afraid that this is an official call. There's something you will want to know about.'

'Don't bet on it, love. I'm having a bitch of a day.' The sergeant looked across at the hole containing the bones. 'Literally. What you got?'

'You know that old fellow who was brought in after the break-in?'

Two minutes later, the detective sergeant replaced the phone in his pocket and stared out across the lawn towards the mill.

'Damn,' he said. 'Damn. Damn, damn.'

And realised that he had forgotten to pass on Lorna's message about the night out.

Chapter eleven

Doctor John Hailes walked into the cell at Levton Bridge Police Station and looked at the downcast figure of Josh Fellows sitting on the bench.

'How are you?' asked Hailes.

Josh did not reply. Hailes noticed that he was trembling.

'This man should not be in a police cell,' said the doctor, turning to the uniformed officer standing at the door. 'He's ill.'

'Better take it up with the sergeant,' shrugged the uniform. 'He arrested him.'

'Don't worry, I will,' said the doctor. 'This man is not fit for questioning.'

* * *

A weary Alistair Marshall and PC Steve Norris knocked on the last house in the village and, after a brief, fruitless conversation with the elderly occupant, walked back down to the patrol car parked next to the green.

'Well, that was a waste of time,' said Norris. 'Apart from that bloke who saw the Audi.'

'Might be important, you never know,' said Marshall, getting into the passenger seat. 'Could help us clear up that break-in at Jim Garbutt's place, if nothing else.'

'I guess.'

Norris got into the driver's seat and turned the key in the ignition. He was about to pull away when he spied in his rear view mirror a white Transit van heading down the hill towards them. Glancing round, he saw that it was being driven by Gary Rylance, who waved as he went past.

'Thought he was going to get some sleep,' said Norris.

'So did I. Anyway, come on, I've just remembered that the sarge wants us to do one more thing before we go back to the station.'

Twenty minutes later, they were back on the edge of Levton Bridge, knocking on the door of the grubby terraced house occupied by Lenny Mattocks, with its grimy paintwork and dirty front window. Marshall was about to knock again when the door was opened by Mattocks. Unshaven and tousle-haired, he was dressed in tattered jeans and a threadbare T-shirt.

'What do you want?' he grunted.

'A chat about someone throwing stones at a cottage near Carperby last night.'

'Weren't me.'

'We think it was,' said Marshall, jamming his foot in the door as Mattocks tried to close it. 'Can we come in?'

Mattocks sighed and ushered them into the hallway with its mouldy wallpaper and thin carpet then into the dingy living room where the officers wrinkled their noses at the fetid smell. Mattocks gestured to a couple of ramshackle armchairs.

'We'll stand, thank you,' said Marshall. 'Now, last night? Are you sure it wasn't you up by the cottage? We've got the stones, what do you think forensics will…?'

'It weren't me, I tell you.'

'Listen, Lenny, we're investigating the murder of Hannah Matthews and…'

Mattocks looked alarmed.

'Hey, that weren't nothing to do with me,' he protested.

'No one is saying that it was but we are trying to trace anyone who has been in that area over the past three days.'

Mattocks thought for a few moments.

'So if I admit it was me throwing stones, I ain't in no trouble?' he asked.

'Possibly not.'

'OK,' said Mattocks, 'yes, it were me throwing them stones, she fucked me off, she did, complaining to Mr Harris like that.'

'You sure you weren't up there any other night?' asked Marshall. 'Tuesday, for example?'

Mattock shook his head vigorously. A lock of lank hair flopped over his eyes and he reached up to flick it away. Flecks of dandruff settled on his shoulder.

'Definitely,' he said. 'The lads in the pub, they'll confirm it.'

'Yeah, I bet they will,' said Marshall.

* * *

Matty Gallagher slammed the phone down on his desk and cursed.

'What's wrong?' asked Butterfield, looking up from her paperwork and glancing across the CID room at her sergeant.

'Everything,' grunted Gallagher, reaching for his mug of tea and scowling when he discovered that it was cold. 'That was Narkie Jarvis, an old mate of mine in the Met Burglary Squad. Thought he might be able to put a name to the lads who dumped the car in London.'

'But he can't?'

'He reckons all the villains he knows get a nose bleed north of Watford Gap.'

'Do you think we have enough to charge them with manslaughter if we do catch them?' asked Butterfield.

'Doubt it. The doc reckons Jim's ticker could have pegged out anytime.' Gallagher walked over to the window and stared moodily down into the yard. 'No, can't see a manslaughter charge sticking. Jesus, there'll be hell to pay once word gets round that the old man is dead.'

'Can you really blame them?'

Gallagher looked sharply at her.

'And exactly what does that mean?' he asked.

Butterfield hesitated, regretting making the comment and inwardly rebuking herself for the slip, acutely aware that her loose mouth continually threatened her intention to reform. It was not as if the sergeant had not warned her before about thinking before speaking. It had become his mantra in his role as her mentor.

'Go on,' said Gallagher, noting her hesitation. 'Spit it out. Besides, you've said it now. The damage is done. Again.'

'It's just,' said Butterfield, choosing her words carefully this time, 'that some folks round here are kind of set in their ways.'

'Get away. You live and learn, eh?'

'I'm not saying they are right, Sarge,' she said quickly, 'far from it, but they do get suspicious about folks who are... different.'

'Different? How?'

'Well, they talk different for a start.'

'I talk different,' said Gallagher.

'Yeah, and you should hear what some of them say about you.' The comment was out before she could stop herself and she clapped a hand to her mouth. 'Sorry, I did not mean to...'

Her voice tailed off. Gallagher watched her growing confusion and found his irritation banished by the constable's forlorn demeanour.

'Blimey, the look on your boat,' he said with a half-smile. 'Just get down those apples and pears and get me a cup of Rosy Lea, will you? And this time try to half-inch some Acker Bilk, yeah?'

Butterfield stared at him for a few bewildered moments.

'Acker Bilk?' she said.

The sergeant roared with laughter.

'Come on,' he said, grabbing his coat from the back of his chair and heading for the door, 'let's go and see what Josh Fellows has got to say for himself. Try and work out what planet he's living on today.'

Gallagher was about to walk into the corridor when one of the phones in the CID room rang. He sighed and ducked back into the room.

'No rest for the wicked,' he said, picking it up.

'Hi, Matty,' said a man's voice. 'I am afraid you have a delegation at reception. They've heard about Jim Garbutt's death.'

Five minutes later, Gallagher found himself sitting in the reception area interview room opposite three people, a white-haired man in a tweed jacket, a severe-looking woman in a duffle coat and the local vicar. Assuming from his uncomfortable demeanour that the vicar had been dragged along purely for moral support, Gallagher switched his attention instead to the older man and the woman. Although the sergeant had not met parish vice-chair Elspeth Gorman before, he had had dealings with Joseph Raleigh, the chairman, when a flasher accosted his wife in the park. The sergeant had always found him brusque and dismissive of police efforts.

For his part, Raleigh did not seem impressed to see the detective either.

'I was rather hoping to speak to DCI Harris,' said Raleigh. 'I usually see him.'

'Yes, well, I am afraid that he is out on inquiries.'

'You'll have to do, I suppose,' sniffed Raleigh. 'It's not ideal talking to a junior officer, though.'

Gallagher looked balefully at him; he had grown tired of people doubting his abilities. However, he said nothing.

'Do I assume that these inquiries of the DCI are in connection with the murder?' asked Raleigh.

'They are.'

'That is partly why we are here, Sergeant. Am I right in thinking that you do not think that Josh Fellows killed the girl?'

'Well, I am not really sure that I can speculate at this…'

'You do not need to,' said Raleigh, 'we have already been told as such and, if that is the case, it does rather indicate that the killer came from outside the area, does it not? And, given that you are digging up the garden at the mill, one could perhaps assume that you are investigating more than one murder?'

'Well, like I say, it's probably too early to speculate…'

'The radio suggested that it is a significant line of inquiry for you,' said Elspeth Gorman, speaking for the first time. 'Are they wrong?'

'Well, you should not believe…'

'And am I also correct,' said Raleigh, interrupting him, 'that Jim Garbutt has died?'

Gallagher knew where this was going; had known the moment he heard that they were there. The moment Julie told him that the old fellow was dead.

'Unfortunately, Jim has died, yes,' he said, choosing his words carefully, 'and, yes, we believe that there is a good chance that the perpetrators came from London but…'

'Look, Sergeant,' said Raleigh, 'there is a lot of anger within the community about criminals using this area to commit offences. It happens time and time again and now two people are dead, probably more than that. People want to know what you are doing about it.'

'We are doing everything in our power to bring…'

'Oh, tosh, man,' exclaimed Raleigh. 'That kind of mealy-mouthed flannel may have worked in your last job but your London ways won't wash with people around here.'

Gallagher thought of the crowd gathered outside the doctor's surgery when Jim Garbutt was taken away, heard again their dark murmurings.

'No,' he said, 'I don't imagine that it will.'

As the sergeant escorted them out of the building, John Hailes emerged into the reception area from the door behind the desk sergeant.

'Just the man,' said the doctor, walking over to Gallagher. 'I have just examined Josh Fellows. There is no way you can interview him.'

'But I've got to interview him.'

'Josh Fellows is a fragile young man and I'm going to ring the hospital to see what they know about him.'

'By all means do that but in the meantime…'

'Listen, Sergeant,' said Hailes, 'that man should not be questioned. Your actions are heavy-handed in the extreme.'

'What do you expect me to do when the bloke has confessed?'

'Look, if he did those horrible things to those girls…'

'I did not say that,' replied Gallagher. 'All I said is that we have to question him.'

'You don't think he did kill them then?'

'I'm not sure. Probably not.'

'Well, we still have to be careful,' said the doctor. 'He is exhibiting signs of serious mental illness and you should proceed with the greatest of caution. Who knows what this young man is capable of doing.'

Gallagher did not reply. He had heard enough people telling him what to think for one day.

Chapter twelve

'I am sorry for what happened to your daughter,' said Jack Harris, looking at the tearful woman sitting on the chair, 'and I can assure you that we will do everything in our power to find whoever did this.'

Angela Matthews nodded but said nothing, instead dabbing at bloodshot eyes with her handkerchief. They were in one of the stuffy little bedrooms in a b. & b. just around the corner from the police station, the chief inspector perched on the edge of the bed, Gillian Roberts standing by the door and in the other chair a blonde woman with a striking resemblance to Hannah Matthews. Her older sister. It was she who spoke.

'They tell me that you have arrested someone,' said Janice Frampton quietly. 'Is that true, Chief Inspector? Have you got the man who did this?'

'It's true that we have arrested someone, yes,' nodded the detective, 'but not true that he is the man who killed your sister, I am afraid.'

'Then why have you arrested him?'

'Let's just say that he is a very troubled young man.'

'Did he admit to killing Hannah?' asked Janice.

Harris hesitated.

'Well?' she said. 'Did he?'

'He did, yes,' said Harris eventually.

'But you don't believe him?'

'I wish I could tell you that I do but, to be honest, I think that he would admit to anything if you asked him.'

'I don't understand,' said Janice. 'Why would he do a thing like that?'

Harris tried to look sympathetic in the face of her bewilderment.

'I know it's difficult to understand,' he said, 'but some people confess to things for no good reason. It's a kind of compulsion with them. He wouldn't be the first to admit to something he has not done. Some people have served years in jail because of it.'

Janice contemplated the comment for a few moments and eventually nodded her acceptance.

'You read about it, I suppose,' she said. 'Even so, can you tell us his name? Are you allowed to do that?'

'As long as you do not tell anyone else. However, it would help us rule him out of our inquiries. He's called Josh Fellows. He lives in the village close to where your sister's body was found.'

Neither woman reacted to the name but Harris had not expected them to. The chief inspector had long since concluded that Josh Fellows's murders had only taken place in the gardens of his diseased mind and that talk of a serial killer stalking the northern hills was fanciful. The dogs' bones in the makeshift grave had only served to crystallise his thinking on the subject. What worried him most was that even the words 'serial killer' changed all the rules. Commanders became twitchy, chief constables demanded instant answers and journalists spied sensational deadlines and found themselves driven to turn scraps of information into stories under the constant pressure from newsdesks seeking new angles. The Press Office was already being besieged by calls from the media seeking comments on the many rumours circulating among the community. It was in everyone's interest that Hannah Matthews be the only victim of the killer, thought Harris.

Silence settled on the room and Harris watched as Angela Matthews started to sob again. Experience had taught the inspector – just like it had taught every detective who had ever investigated a murder – that most killings were committed by people close to the victims rather than deranged slayers prowling the night. Of course, he knew that there were predators out there but, sitting in the stuffy bedroom and surveying Angela, the detective chief inspector wondered what secrets Hannah Matthews had been keeping from her family. And how he was going to ask the question with the mother in this state. The sister, he decided, she was the one to talk to.

Before the inspector could make his mind up about how to proceed, Gillian Roberts came to sit on the bed and reached out to hold Angela's hand.

'I'm sorry,' mumbled Angela, the tears flowing harder now.

'It's ok, luvvie, you let it all out,' said Roberts. 'Like DCI Harris says, we'll get whoever did this to your daughter.'

Harris frowned, acutely conscious that he did not feel as confident as the detective inspector. He had always avoided making promises that he did not know he could keep. Without realising he had done, he shook his head. Experience had taught him that, unless you achieved a breakthrough in the first twenty-four hours of murder inquiries, they had a tendency to drag on into days, weeks and even months. Sometimes years, sometimes never. Sitting in the stuffy little bedroom, Jack Harris felt a long way from a breakthrough.

* * *

Matty Gallagher and Alison Butterfield felt the same sense of frustration as they sat in the interview room two hundred metres away at Levton Bridge Police Station and looked gloomily across the desk at the duty solicitor then at the hunched figure of Josh Fellows. He had not spoken since being brought up from the cells following the visit from the doctor. After John Hailes had hurried back to his surgery, Gallagher had phoned Harris, who had overridden the doctor's suggestion that the interview be delayed, adding 'if only for the sake of the flowerbeds'. Sitting and surveying the prisoner now, Gallagher was not so sure it was a good idea and resolved not to press him.

'We're not going to find anyone buried at the mill, are we?' asked the sergeant gently, staring at Fellows until the sense that the detective's eyes were upon him made Josh raise his head.

Gallagher eyed him with concern then glanced at Butterfield. Gallagher could see that the detective constable was similarly worried about the lifeless expression on the prisoner's face, an overwhelming sensation that behind the eyes lay only a void. Wishing he had remonstrated harder with the DCI, Gallagher wondered if he should call off the interview. However, the duty solicitor did not look concerned and the thought of the officers continuing to dig up the mill house garden cautioned the sergeant against abandonment.

'Come on, Josh,' continued Gallagher, 'we're digging that lovely garden up, the garden you did so much to create, for nothing. There's no girls and we both know it.'

'They're there,' said Josh, infused with a sudden vigour, the first time he had spoken since entering the room. 'Where I buried them. Eight of them. They dance for me.'

'They *dance* for you?'

'Yes, every night, they dance for me.' Josh smiled and his face assumed a far-off expression.

'Maybe you ought to think carefully about what you are saying,' said the solicitor.

'No, I want to tell them,' said Josh. 'When the music comes they dance for me. Out on the lawn. It's beautiful.

They're beautiful. Always smiling.' He looked at the sergeant. 'You've been there, didn't you hear the music?'

Gallagher recalled the faint strains of music that he fancied he had heard as he stood in the garden but he quickly rebuked himself silently for such fanciful notions. Nevertheless, the thought troubled him.

'I don't doubt that you think they dance for you,' he said, noting that Josh's eyes were glistening with tears, 'but I am afraid I don't think they're real.'

'They are! I killed them and put them there. In the ground. You have just not found them yet.'

'Including Hannah Matthews?'

Josh hesitated but said nothing.

'Because you know where we found her, don't you?' continued the sergeant. 'You saw where we found her so there is no way that you could have buried her in the garden, is there? She can't be in two places at once.'

'OK, maybe not her but I killed the others.' The voice had lost its energy now. More of a mumble. 'I'm a murderer, that's what I am. A killer.'

The solicitor leaned forward in his chair and looked as if he was about to intervene again but something stopped him and he sat back, nodding at the detective to continue.

'Did you find the bones?' asked Josh before either of the detectives could speak. 'Down by the lake? Did you find the bones?'

'We did, yes, but they belong to a dog.'

'No, they don't.'

'The pathologist says that they do.'

'Well, he's wrong.'

Gallagher was about to remonstrate with Josh but something about his resolute expression made him think better of the idea. Instead, the sergeant glanced at Butterfield, who shrugged.

* * *

'I am sure that Jack Harris knows what he is doing,' said Philip Curtis, fielding the sixth telephone call from the chief constable's office that day.

The district commander reached out to straighten the pile of papers on his desk as the chief's staff officer continued to talk.

'Yes, I know the media have descended on the place.' Curtis glanced over to the television mounted on the wall in the corner of the room, which showed a reporter clutching a microphone and standing at the front gates to the mill house, now shrouded from view amidst the gathering afternoon mist. The reporter was interviewing parish council chairman Joseph Raleigh. 'I know Sky are running pictures of us digging in the garden but I am sure that Harris would not let it happen unless they had good reason.'

He reached out to straighten the papers again.

'No, of course this line about a serial killer did not come from us,' he said. 'Oh, come on, talk sense. You know how it is up here when the rumour mill gets going. In fact, Jack Harris went out of his way to caution the media against using the phrase. Yes, I know he did not complete the media training course but that does not...'

The commander was not given time to finish and after listening for a further minute during which he hardly spoke, he sighed, replaced the receiver and stared out of his window into the deepening gloom of the afternoon.

* * *

Sitting opposite Josh Fellows in the interview room, Matty Gallagher had no idea what to say next and the knock on the door came as a relief. He turned to see the door open and Alistair Marshall beckoning for the sergeant to join him in the corridor.

'What you got, Alistair?' asked Gallagher, walking out of the room and closing the door behind him. 'And it had better be good because we're getting nowhere in there. The lad's off his rocker.'

'Officially.'

'What?'

'He's officially a fruit loop. Dr Hailes has just been on. Says he really has to insist that you stop interviewing the kid.'

'Why?'

'Roxham General knew all about Josh Fellows. He's been under one of their shrinks for the best part of twenty years. Started when he started acting funny at primary school. Talking to imaginary friends, that sort of thing.'

'We all did that.'

'Yes, but there was more to it with Josh Fellows. He never really grew out of it.' Alistair Marshall looked down at his notebook. 'They told him to do things.'

'Things?'

'Seems that when he was in his last weeks at primary school, he broke into the school's pets area one lunchtime and strangled one of the guinea pigs. The teachers found him trying to set fire to the gerbils.'

'He did what?'

'Apparently, another one of the guinea pigs met a similar untimely end a few weeks earlier – it was all over the local paper. Staff had assumed that it was down to vandals but it looks like it was young Josh Fellows.'

'Did he get prosecuted?'

'Got sent to the shrink instead.' Alistair consulted his notebook again. 'Didn't do him much good. He had spells in a psychiatric hospital when he was fifteen, then again when he was twenty. He was clear for five years but it all flared up again recently. He was referred by his mother after he started talking to people in the back garden, except there was nobody there.'

'Except they were. I think Josh Fellows saw them just like he sees girls dancing on the lawn.'

'You could be right,' said the detective constable, glancing at his notebook once more. 'According to the hospital, Josh had another spell locked up before being released again a few weeks ago. It seems he may not have been taking his medication. The kid's a looney tunes.'

'In more ways than one,' said the sergeant, recalling the faint sound of music drifting across the gardens earlier in the day. 'I am not sure that today can get any worse.'

'Oh ye of little faith.'

Gallagher looked bleakly at the detective constable.

'Why don't I want to hear this?' he asked.

'Sorry, Sarge. The owner of the mill has been on from London. Says he has just seen some pictures on Sky and wants to remind you that when he gave us permission to search the gardens, he expressly said "no mess".'

Gallagher visualised the scarred and pitted garden.

'Well, that ain't happening,' he said. 'Even Monty Don would struggle to put that little lot back together. Hey, perhaps it's Nigel in the hole.'

'Nigel?'

'His dog.'

'You need to get out more,' said Alistair. 'Anyway, the guy wants you to ring him. He said something about compensation for all the damage we've caused.'

'Can't Jack Harris talk to him instead?'

'He's down at reception talking to that mad woman that keeps banging on about foxes.'

'Maybe my day's not so bad after all,' said the sergeant, pushing his way back into the interview room where he looked at the solicitor. 'Something tells me that this would be a good time to call a halt.'

'I think you're probably right,' said the lawyer.

* * *

Watched by John Hailes from the top of the police station steps, two uniformed officers helped a dazed-looking Josh Fellows into a patrol vehicle. The doctor glanced at Matty Gallagher, who was standing next to him.

'It's for the best,' said Hailes. 'He is a very disturbed young man. I feel happier with him off the streets but he needs to be in hospital, not in one of your cells.'

112

Gallagher watched the car head down the hill. 'Maybe,' he said.

Chapter thirteen

'Thank you for coming forward,' said Harris, staring across the interview room desk at Jenny Meynell then glancing at Gillian Roberts, who was sitting next to him. 'The detective inspector tells me that you may have some important information relating to the death of Hannah Matthews.'

'I am here only reluctantly, Chief Inspector.'

'That makes a change. Normally you can't wait to bend my ear.'

The comment earned him a glare.

'I am only here,' she said tartly, 'because you would find out eventually. No point in keeping it from you, is there?'

'Never a good policy, Miss Meynell. Mind, I do find it rather remarkable that you know the young woman whose body turns up so close to your home in the middle of nowhere. How come?'

'Because I taught her.'

'So the detective inspector tells me. Where exactly was this?'

'Laurel Primary School in Redbridge. I assumed that you made the connection after my slip when we talked in this room a couple of days ago.'

Harris remembered her nervous reaction when she mentioned Redbridge during the conversation.

'A slip indeed,' said Harris without knowing why except that he felt the sudden need to appear in command of a situation that he sensed was spiralling out of his control. There was clearly much he did not know. Jack Harris had never liked secrets and Jenny Meynell had the air of a woman with plenty of them.

'Hannah was a nice girl,' said Jenny sadly. 'Good parents. They weren't all like that. Some parents were extremely unpleasant to deal with.'

She hesitated, her features darkening and the officers gave her time to elaborate on the comment but she did not.

'Something you want to tell us?' asked Harris.

'No.' The barrier had gone up again.

'Hannah was in your class then?' said the inspector.

'Yes. She was very chatty. Always stayed back to help me tidy up. She was in the Brownie pack that I ran as well. Down at the local church hall.' Jenny shook her head. 'Such a waste, such a terrible waste.'

'And were you aware that she had moved up to Manchester?'

'Oh, yes.'

'How?' Harris fixed her with one of his looks. Although he still did not understand what was happening, pieces were starting to fall into place and his suspicions were hardening. 'How did you know that she had come up to the Manchester area?'

'Facebook.'

'And why would you follow her on Facebook? You must have had hundreds of pupils in your time. Why her?'

'I follow quite a few of my former pupils, Chief Inspector. A lot of teachers do it. We like to know how they have got on in life. One of my old pupils is an Oxford University professor, another works in Milan in the fashion industry and…'

'And Hannah Matthews ended up lying in a muddy ditch with her head stoved in,' said the inspector. There was an edge to his voice now. 'And, of all the places in the world, she turns up close to your cottage. That's one hell of a coincidence, is it not?'

'What are you suggesting?' she asked, eyes flashing defiance. 'I hope you do not think that I was in any way involved in the death of this unfortunate…'

'Let me level with you, Miss Meynell.' The inspector's voice was harsh now. Almost accusing. 'I think that you know a lot more than you are letting on. Time to end this ridiculous charade and start…'

'Like I said, I am prepared to confirm that I knew Hannah only because you would have found out.' She crossed her arms and sat back in her chair. 'However, beyond that, I am simply not permitted to divulge…'

'Permitted to divulge!' exclaimed Harris angrily, banging the desk with his fist. 'Permitted to fucking divulge! Listen, I have a chief constable who's ringing my commander every ten minutes demanding to know why I'm digging up a perfectly good garden, half the people in the valley are convinced that they're going to be murdered in their beds tonight by some rampaging serial killer and the media are after my hide so you had better start talking, lady!'

'It's supposed to be a secret,' said Jenny Meynell, retaining her composure in the face of the inspector's angry outburst. 'That's how it works.'

'How what works?' asked Harris, his anger abating as quickly as it had flared, to be replaced by bewilderment. That familiar sense of a situation spiralling out of control returned.

'I am saying nothing more,' said Jenny Meynell defiantly. 'I have already told you too much.'

'I'm not sure you have told us anything.'

'Well, it's all you are going to get out of me. I know the rules, Chief Inspector.'

'Rules? What rules?'

Jenny Meynell shook her head and did not reply.

'No,' she said.

Harris glanced at his bemused detective inspector, who shrugged. A minute later, the two detectives walked out into the reception area, closing the interview room door behind them.

'What do you make of that, Gillian?' asked Harris, leaning with his back against the wall. 'Because I have not got the foggiest what she is talking about.'

'I am not sure that I have ever heard anything quite like it.'

'What do you think she means by all this not permitted to divulge stuff? Permitted by whom? And what rules? Whose rules?' Harris scowled. 'I thought I made the bloody rules round here.'

Before Roberts could reply, Harris's mobile phone rang. He removed the device from his jacket pocket and looked down at the caller's name. Leckie.

'Don't tell me, Graham,' he grunted, taking the call, 'you have found half a dozen missing women that I never knew existed because I binned the memo about our friendly neighbourhood maniac?'

'Just the one actually.'

'Why the hell has everyone started talking in riddles?'

'Let me make it a bit clearer for you,' said Leckie. 'See, after you mentioned that woman and her foxes, I did a couple of checks. Just topping and tailing things, to be honest, making sure I hadn't missed anything. Old habits die hard. Didn't really expect to find anything on your Jenny Meynell…'

'But you did?'

'Boy, did I, matey. She's a woman with a nifty line in enemies.'

Five minutes later, Harris ended the call and stared at the detective inspector, who had been watching him in bemusement, trying to glean what he had been talking about from his occasional exclamations.

'Enemies?' she said. 'Gangsters? What on earth has Leckie turned up?'

Harris looked back at the door to the interview room.

'You'll never believe who we've got in there,' he said with a shake of the head. 'You really won't.'

'I am assuming it's more than a mad woman who has a thing about foxes?'

'Too right,' said Harris and pushed his way back into the interview room, followed by an intrigued Roberts.

'Can I go now?' asked Jenny Meynell hopefully, looking up. 'I really would like to go.'

'I am afraid that is not going to be possible.' The inspector sat down at the table and eyed her intently. 'You have got an awful lot of explaining to do, I think.'

'I told you, according to the rules…'

'Yes, yes, yes, I know all about the rules.'

'You do?' She looked at him uneasily.

'I do but as I was just reminding the detective inspector, I make the rules around here.'

'Now listen here…' began Jenny.

'No, you listen. If you are determined to keep playing your little game, so be it, but how about we ask Esmee Colclough instead? What do you think?'

The effect was dramatic. The colour drained from Jenny Meynell's face and she stared at him in horror. Gillian Roberts viewed the transformation in amazement then looked at Harris, who was now thoroughly enjoying himself. Finally, thought the inspector, and for the first time that day, he was in control and his old sense of confidence came flooding back.

'So,' he repeated, 'what *would* dear Esmee have to say for herself, do you think?'

'Is someone going to explain what is happening?' asked Roberts. 'Who the hell is Esmee Colclough?'

Harris looked at Jenny.

'Care to tell her?' he said. 'Or should I?'

'How did you find out?' asked Jenny in a voice that was barely audible. 'How on earth do you know? It's supposed to be a secret.'

'I told you not to keep secrets from me. I always find out in the end.' The inspector fixed her with a stare. 'Right, let's start playing by my rules, shall we?'

Defeated, Esmee Colclough nodded.

Chapter fourteen

'Witness Protection!' exclaimed Philip Curtis, staring across his desk at Harris in astonishment. 'Jenny Meynell is in Witness Protection?'

'Sure is,' said Harris, reaching for his mug of tea and giving a half-smile, enjoying the district commander's reaction. 'As my doughty sergeant would doubtless say, "would you Adam and Eve it?"'

'Well, she's got a funny way of staying low profile, that's all I can say,' grunted the commander. 'Half the bloody valley knows about her damned fool fox story. Are you sure someone is not spinning you some sort of line?'

'I wish they were but it all checks out. New identity, new home, the lot. Witness Protection confirmed it all. Apparently, she told her friends that she'd come into some money and was going to live on the Welsh coast. Came north instead.'

'Why here?'

'She knows the area from when she was a kid. Came up on family holidays. They used to stay at a b. & b. in town – ironically enough, it's the one we've put Hannah Matthews's family in.'

'Witness Protection,' said the district commander, shaking his head in disbelief. 'So much for blending into the background. The woman has been nothing but trouble since she arrived.'

'Hey, you don't have to tell me. I'm the one who has had to listen to her banging on about it, remember. Anyway, Witness Protection were pretty hacked off when I told them how she's been behaving.'

'I'll bet they were.'

'The DCI there said they'd been in two minds about putting her in the programme in the first place because she's such a crackerjack,' said Harris, taking a gulp of tea. 'However, like he said, needs must when the Devil drives. And she's picked herself one heck of a Devil has our Jenny Meynell – or Esmee Colclough as we should now call her. A real heavyweight in the London gangland scene.'

'How on earth does a primary school teacher from Redbridge get herself tangled up in something like this in the first place?' asked Curtis. 'She seems like such an innocuous person.'

'Not sure that's the word I would use to describe her. Anyway, once you get into it, things start to make sense and it might just lead us to the person who killed young Hannah Matthews.'

* * *

'So, I rang the DCI at Witness Protection,' said Harris, sipping at another mug of tea as he and Gallagher sat in the inspector's office. 'It all started when our Esmee married a guy called James Colclough ten years ago. James set up a bathroom fittings shop in London and did well for himself. Started splashing the cash. Developed a weakness for late-night card games and got himself into debt to some local nasties.'

'Never a good idea,' said Gallagher. 'How much did he owe them?'

'Thick end of ten grand. They used the debt to force him to use the shop as a front for stolen goods.'

'Hardly the kind of stuff to get you placed in Witness Protection, surely?' said Gallagher. 'A few knock-off taps.'

'But it did bring him into the sphere of a gangland figure going by the name of Thomas Ross.'

Gallagher gave a low whistle.

'You know him?' asked Harris.

'Everyone in the Met knows Tommy Ross,' said Gallagher. 'Nasty piece of work. Razor Ross, they call him.'

'How imaginative,' murmured Harris.

'Imaginative or not, you don't cross him. So where does the fragrant Tommy fit into the picture?'

'Apparently, he used his ill-gotten gains to buy a nice house in an upmarket area of Redbridge. Mock-Tudor, big gardens, high wall round it, even a couple of peacocks.'

'Wasted on the likes of him.'

'Probably so, but it did mean that he got to send his kid to the best primary school in the area. Ross's daughter seems to have taken after her father, throwing her weight around, bullying the other kids, always being lippy in class. And you can probably guess who her class teacher was.'

'Esmee Colclough.'

'The very same. One day the kid goes too far, bites a classmate and unleashes a host of profanities at our Esmee when she tries to take her to the headteacher. You can imagine how Esmee reacted to that.'

'Not well.'

'Exactly. She tells the kid off, there's an unholy row and the kid claims that Esmee slapped her. Next thing Esmee knows, Tommy Ross is in her classroom effing and blinding. Our Esmee, feisty to the end, you have to admire her spirit if nothing else, refuses to apologise. A couple of the other kids confirm that she did not lay a finger on her and the headteacher backs her up. Tommy is livid. Sees it as damaging his hard-man reputation.'

'He does not appreciate folks standing up to him.'

'Clearly not because he gives Esmee a week to quit her job. When she doesn't, he gets some of his heavies to put her house windows out as a taster.'

'Sounds like his style,' said Gallagher. 'So what happened next?'

'Esmee's husband had seen enough. Witness Protection reckon he's probably still running. The local cops hear what's happening and approach Esmee with an offer – stand up in court and say what James told her about Ross and they'll spirit her away on Witness Protection, give her the dream life in the hills she always wanted. Make hubby the same offer if they ever catch him.'

'It does make you wonder if the lads that screwed Jim Garbutt's gaff might have been looking for her. Maybe the break-in was just old habits dying hard.'

'My thoughts exactly. Not many people around. Remote houses.' Harris gave his sergeant a sly look. 'A woollyback police force that struggles to get the lid off a Biro. What could be better, eh?'

'Indeed,' grinned Gallagher. 'Hang on, though, we know they went back to Redbridge without her.'

'How about this? Esmee followed Hannah on Facebook. What if Esmee got lonely and broke the rules? Contacted the kid. Asked her to come and talk about the good old days. Hannah sees the lads near Esmee's cottage, they panic, think she can identify them, kill her then flee back down south. Fancy a trip to your old stomping ground?'

'What, meet up with some of the Met boys?' beamed Gallagher.

'Take Alistair if you want. The experience will do him good. I'd like you to come with me to see Hannah's family before you go, though.'

'Sure,' said the sergeant as they stood up. 'What happens to Esmee now?'

'Ironically, it turns out she had played them a bit and did not know as much as she let on but by then they were stuck with the mad old chuff. Witness Protection are sending someone to pick her up. I want that woman as far away from here as possible.'

'Amen to that,' said Gallagher.

* * *

Jack Harris tapped gently on the bedroom door at the b. & b. It was answered by Janice Frampton. Her eyes were heavy-lidded and they could see that she had been crying.

'Inspector,' she said, 'my mother is sleeping if you were hoping to…'

'No, I am happy to talk to you, Janice,' said Harris. 'Would you like to go down to the lounge for a cup of tea? I'm sure Betty will do us a brew. Oh, can I introduce you to Sergeant Gallagher.'

'Hello,' said Gallagher, showing her his warrant card. 'I am very sorry for your loss, really I am.'

'You're not from round here,' said Janice as she slipped out of the room and they walked down the corridor.

'I'm from Bermondsey,' said the sergeant.

'I know it well,' said Janice as they headed down the stairs. 'We lived there before moving to Redbridge.'

'Small world,' said Gallagher.

A few minutes later, the three of them were sitting amid the swirling wallpaper of the lounge, nursing cups of tea, Harris acutely conscious that he had drunk three in less than an hour and wishing the pressure on his bladder would ease.

'How can I help you?' asked Janice. 'Is it about the man you arrested? Have you changed your mind, Chief Inspector? Do you think that he killed my sister?'

'Nothing has changed. I wanted to talk about something else. Run another name past you. Esmee Colclough. She's a teacher.'

'What on earth has Miss Colclough got to do with my sister's death?'

'If I tell you, you must keep this to yourself. Promise?'

She nodded, startled by his intensity.

'I promise,' she said. 'What's this about, Chief Inspector?'

'We wonder if your sister could have been on her way to see Esmee when she was attacked?'

'But Esmee Colclough lives in London, surely?'

'*Did* live in London. She moved here a few weeks ago, and we believe that they may have been in touch recently. In the past few days.'

'They sent messages to each other on Facebook,' explained Gallagher, pulling a crumpled print-out from his jacket pocket and scanning the contents. 'Twice last week and once the day before your sister was murdered.'

'But why would they do that? Neither of us had seen Esmee Colclough for the best part of ten years.'

'That's what we want to find out,' said Harris. 'One of the Facebook contacts between your sister and Esmee appears to have involved them swapping phone numbers so we wonder if they were planning to meet up.'

'She never mentioned it. Mind, I had not talked to her for a few days. My son has been unwell with a virus so we'd been a bit preoccupied. I'm sorry but…'

'They did agree to meet,' said a voice and the detectives turned to see Hannah's mother standing at the door.

She looked pale and her eyes were even more bloodshot than before. She walked over and sat down heavily on one of the sofas.

'They did?' asked Harris.

'I didn't think anything of it because she did not tell me that Esmee lived up here,' continued Angela, walking over to sit heavily in one of the armchairs. 'I just assumed that she was going to London to see her. Hannah had friends in London, I thought she would make a weekend of it.'

'Why did they agree to meet after all this time?' asked Harris.

'I don't know. Hannah was a bit vague about it.' Angela looked hard at the inspector. 'Is Esmee Colclough why my daughter died, Chief Inspector?'

'Well, I am not sure I would go that far.'

'But if they had not agreed to meet, she would still be alive today?'

Harris thought for a few moments.

'I am afraid,' he said, 'that might well be the case.'

Chapter fifteen

Darkness was beginning to slide its silky fingers around the northern hills once more when a weary Matty Gallagher guided his car through the gathered media, ignoring the flash of the cameras, and up the drive to the mill house. Parking, he got out of the vehicle and walked down the drive and across the lawn to where a group of uniformed officers in dark blue overalls were standing on the edge of the lake, chatting, a couple of them smoking cigarettes. Their shovels lay nearby, caked thick with mud.

'All done?' asked Gallagher.

'For today,' said one of them. 'May need to be back tomorrow. Depends on you really, Matty.'

'Show me what you have found.'

The officer led the sergeant round the fringes of the lake, fishing a torch from his overalls pocket and pointing the beam in turn to eight holes, in the bottom of each one the detective could see collections of bones.

'Are they all dogs?' asked Gallagher.

'Ask Barbara Woodhouse over there,' said the uniform, pointing to a young man in a light anorak, who was standing by the water's edge.

'Who he?'

'Alan Bradham. Just started in the vets at Yafforth. Bit wet behind the ears but he seems to know his stuff.'

Gallagher walked over to the young man.

'Mr Bradham,' said the sergeant, extending a hand in welcome, 'I'm Matthew Gallagher from Levton Bridge CID. Are they all dogs then?'

'Yes, there's no doubt about that,' said the young man sadly, shaking his hand. 'This is very disturbing indeed.'

'Tell me about it,' murmured the sergeant. 'I take it they did not die natural deaths?'

'I've only done a cursory inspection but I'd say they were strangled. Whoever did it used considerable force and I do not think death would have been particularly quick.'

'So much for dancing girls,' said Gallagher.

The vet looked bewildered.

'Dancing girls?' he said.

'Believe me,' replied Gallagher. 'You really do not want to know.'

* * *

Shortly after six that evening, Jack Harris eyed with distaste the dishevelled fat man sitting opposite him in the stuffy little interview room at Levton Bridge Police Station. For Harris, the early start to the day was beginning to catch up with him and his fatigued mood was not helped by the pungent odour emanating from the man sitting opposite him.

Aged in his mid-thirties and dressed in a threadbare jumper and tattered jeans, Andy Gaylard was the last of the local sex offenders to be interviewed by Harris that afternoon. Gillian Roberts had offered to provide someone else to do it but the DCI had opted to carry out the interviews himself, explaining, 'I told the media that our killer was not local and I want to look this lot in the eyes to make damn sure I'm right.'

Harris, who had only limited dealings with Gaylard, glanced down at the top file on the desk.

'You're quite a little darling, aren't you?' he said.

Sweat glistened on Gaylard's brow.

'I don't know what you mean,' he said.

'Spying on teenage girls in the changing room at Roxham swimming baths, groping a fourteen-year-old on the bus,' said Harris, running a finger down the record sheet. 'Flashing in the park here. And again. Oh, and again. To the wife of the parish council chairman, no less. My, my, you are a busy boy.'

Harris sat back in his chair and surveyed Gaylard without much enthusiasm. Gaylard, for his part, returned the inspector's gaze with trepidation. A petty serial offender down the years, he had no reason to like or trust the police, and certainly not Jack Harris. Everyone knew that Harris hated sex pests, especially when they transgressed on his patch. Having previously only been interviewed by other officers, Gaylard's blood had run cold when uniform had called at his rented terraced house on the edge of Levton Bridge and told him that the detective chief inspector wanted to speak to him.

'I ain't done nothing wrong,' said Gaylard, unnerved by the inspector's silence.

'I very much doubt that to be the case.'

'I've been keeping my nose clean.'

'Hopefully it's not the only thing that you've been keeping clean.'

'What's this about, Mr Harris?' protested Gaylard. 'I ain't in no trouble. I told Mr Gallagher I wouldn't do no more flashing and I've been as good as my word.'

'Hannah Matthews,' said the inspector. 'Heard of her?'

'What, the girl they found in the field?' said Gaylard, going pale. 'Now hang on, Mr Harris, that ain't nothing to do with me. You ain't pinning that on me.'

'Are you suggesting that I would fabricate evidence?' Steel in the voice.

Gaylard looked alarmed. 'No, no, of course not.'

'Good, because if you were, you and me would fall out pretty quickly. Where were you on Tuesday night?'

'At home. On the computer.'

'I'm sure you were. Anyone verify that?'

Gaylard shook his head.

'I live alone.'

'Of course you do.' Overcome with fatigue, Harris gave Gaylard a final scornful look, pushed the file away and nodded at the uniformed officer standing by the door. 'Get him out of my sight, will you?'

A relieved Gaylard having gone, Harris sat for a few moments and closed his eyes then opened them again to look once more at the rap sheet. Had he missed anything? With Gaylard? With any of them? Harris felt the return of the twinges of doubt that had assailed him for much of the day. He felt like someone trying to complete a jigsaw without the final piece. Without, if he was honest, a lot of the other pieces as well. Closing the file, he shook his head just as Gillian Roberts entered the room, wrinkling her nose at the smell.

'Don't tell me,' she said. 'Andy Gaylard?'

'The very same.'

'Thought so, I'd recognise his Cologne anywhere. A touch more sweet and sickly than Benny Lowery's, I always find. Less Eau de Groin.' She sat down at the desk and grinned as Harris chuckled. 'Anything interesting?'

'Neither Lowery or Gaylard have it in them to kill. Nor,' and Harris picked up another file, 'does Michael Todd. They may be sleaze-balls but there's no way they murdered Hannah Matthews. Same for our stone-thrower Lenny Mattocks. Have the lads gone to London?'

'Traffic have just taken them down to Roxham to catch the train. Oh, and we've just heard from the General, they've got no beds on the psych ward so they have sent Josh to stay at a secure centre in Carlisle.'

'Maybe it's for the best.'

'You pretty sure he's not our guy then?'

'As sure as I can be. He's no danger to anyone, unless you're a dog.' Harris thought of his own dogs dozing underneath the radiator back in his office and scowled. 'Mind, that's reason enough to lock him up and throw away the key in my book.'

'There's plenty of cases of murderers who started on animals. Take Ted Bundy. And the RSPCA brought out a report a few years ago saying…'

'Josh Fellows is no Ted Bundy. Mind, I seem to have spent the day being wrong.'

'Don't worry about it, it happens to us all.' Gillian Roberts stood up. 'What I actually came to tell you is that Witness Protection are here for Esmee Colclough. They're at the front counter if you want to say a tender goodbye to her.'

'I take it the search of her cottage came up clean?'

'As a whistle.'

Two minutes later, the detectives were standing in the reception area chatting to the Witness Protection officers. A female uniformed officer brought Esmee Colclough through the door next to the front counter. Esmee walked over to the chief inspector.

'On your way then?' he said.

'Like you care.' That defensive note again.

Harris did not reply. She was right. He didn't care. He had had enough of Esmee Colclough.

'Since we are unlikely to meet again, do you want to change your mind about telling me about Hannah?' he asked. 'Was she on her way to see you the night she was killed?'

'I'm not sure. Perhaps.'

'What does that mean?'

'Look,' and Esmee glanced at the Witness Protection officers and lowered her voice, 'I know that I broke the rules by contacting her on Facebook but I did not invite her to come and see me. To the best of my knowledge, she did not even know where I was. She probably assumed I was still living in London.'

'I think you are lying, Esmee. I think it comes second nature to you. I think you did tell her where you were living.'

Esmee hesitated and yet again her demeanour changed, in the way he had seen so many times in his dealings with her. Gone was the fire, replaced by something more vulnerable.

'I may have let something slip,' she said.

'You're unbelievable.'

Esmee looked uneasily at him.

'I do hope that she did not die on my account, Chief Inspector,' she said.

Harris said nothing. There was no way he was going to give her the satisfaction of absolution. One of the Witness Protection officers walked over and ushered her towards the door.

'I'm sorry,' he said, 'I'm going to have to take her away, assuming you do not need her for anything else?'

'Be my guest.'

'Come on, love,' said the officer, guiding her by the arm, 'we've got a long journey ahead of us.'

As the officer opened the front door to allow her through, Esmee turned back to look hard at the inspector.

'I did try to tell you,' she said accusingly, the fire ignited once more. She jabbed an accusatory finger at him. 'None of you would listen.'

'For the last time,' said Harris forcefully, 'there is no serial killer. I may not be certain about much at the moment but that's one thing I am sure about.'

With a snort of derision, Esmee stepped out into the night. Gillian Roberts winked at the DCI and headed back towards the stairs up to her office. Harris did not follow. Walking over to the front door behind Esmee, he went outside and stood at the top of the steps. Just to be sure, he told himself. He watched as the saloon car with the blacked-out windows reached the top of the bank, its brake lights glowing red in the darkness before the vehicle disappeared into the market place on its way towards the moors road. Harris sighed with relief.

'And don't come back,' he murmured.

The inspector was so focused on the vehicle that he did not initially notice the middle-aged woman in the beige coat standing a few metres in the other direction, further down the hill, watching him intently. When he did turn his attention to her, the inspector noticed that she seemed to be battling strong emotions.

'Can I help you?' asked the detective.

'Chief Inspector Harris?' she asked, her voice tremulous.

'That's me.'

She walked up the steps.

'I've driven more than two hundred miles to see you, Chief Inspector.'

'You have?'

'My name is Geraldine Morris. I heard on the television that you think you might have a serial killer in your area?'

'No, I don't. It's all media speculation. There's no serial killer here, you can take that from me.'

'Then where's my daughter?' she cried, grasping his arm. 'Where is my darling Paula?'

Jack Harris noted the pain in her eyes and the tears glistening on her cheek and thought suddenly of the mill house garden lying silent in the darkness with just a single uniformed officer standing guard over its secrets. He thought also of his pronouncements that had already proved wrong that day. And he thought of Josh Fellows's dancing girls.

'I think,' he said, touching her gently on the arm, 'that you had better come in.'

Chapter sixteen

The chief inspector ushered Geraldine Morris into the interview room by the reception area.

'Take a seat,' he said. 'Would you like a cup of tea?'

She nodded gratefully. 'Please. It's been a long day.'

'It certainly has.' Harris walked out of the room and glanced over to the officer behind the counter. 'Can you do us a couple of teas, please, Bob? Oh, and tell the DI that I could do with her help, will you?'

Five minutes later, the two detectives sat and watched Geraldine Morris as she sipped at her mug of tea and tried to compose herself.

'Tell me about Paula,' said Harris eventually.

Geraldine reached into her handbag and pulled out a colour photograph which she slid across the desk. Harris stared down at the image of a laughing blonde girl posing with a couple of friends in a bar. Wordlessly, he passed it to Roberts, who raised an eyebrow. But for a few small differences, it could easily have been a picture of Hannah Matthews. For reasons that he could not quite rationalise, Jack Harris thought of the pictures he had seen in the books of Ted Bundy's victims. Smiling young women with their lives ahead of them. Then he thought of the dog bones in the garden. The doubts came crowding back.

'Pretty girl,' he said as Roberts handed the picture back to Paula's mother. 'Where was it taken?'

'In Tenerife. She had gone there with some girlfriends to celebrate the end of their finals. It was taken on their last night.'

'What was she studying?' asked Roberts.

'Medicine. She was going to become a GP.'

'When was this taken?'

'Last summer. She had only been back three weeks when she disappeared.' The tears were close now. 'It was a terrible time. Her father took it really badly. She was our only child. He killed himself earlier this year. Left a note saying he could not take it any more. I found him in the car. In the garage.'

Her voice tailed off and the sobbing came harder now and her shoulders hunched as her body was wracked by sobs.

'I'm sorry,' said Harris. It always sounded so lame.

Geraldine nodded but words were beyond her.

'Take your time, luvvie,' said Gillian Roberts, reaching out to pat her hand. 'There's no rush.'

Geraldine nodded her acceptance of the gesture and after a few moments, the tears subsided and she resumed her story.

'Paula had just started a summer job in Vision Express,' she said. 'In Nottingham city centre.'

'Is that where you live?' asked Harris. 'Nottingham?'

She nodded.

'Paula was living at home at the time. She went out to work in the morning, said she would be staying the night with a friend, she did not say who, and she would see me the next day. The store manager rang at about ten, saying she had not turned up for work. She had just vanished.' Geraldine shook her head in disbelief. 'I didn't even have chance to say goodbye.'

She hesitated, fighting the tears.

'I'd been ill and slept in that morning,' she said when she had composed herself. 'When I woke up, she'd gone. Just a note on the kitchen table saying she'd be back at the usual time.'

'Were there no sightings?' asked Harris.

'Not really. The local police were very good. They searched local parks and the river and circulated her picture to the media, and they checked CCTV in shops along the route she normally took. There was one fuzzy image of a girl walking past the park but you couldn't really see who it was. In the end, they told me that she might be dead. Her ATM card had not been used and calls to her mobile just went to answerphone then,' and she hesitated again, fighting the tears once more, 'then the battery went dead.'

Geraldine took a handkerchief out of her bag and started dabbing eyes that glistened with tears.

'I could not believe it when the police said they thought she was dead,' she said. 'Can you imagine what it is like as a mother when you hear that?'

Geraldine looked at Gillian Roberts, who thought of her two boys, doubtless sitting at home in front of the television, bickering over the remote control.

'No,' said the detective inspector, 'no, I can't.'

'Your daughter disappeared in Nottingham,' said Harris. 'What made you drive up here?'

'My darling Paula is out there somewhere and I will never stop looking until I find her. When I saw on the television report that you might have a serial killer, I thought...' Her voice tailed off. 'Hope, it's a terrible thing, Chief Inspector.'

'Look, I don't want to sound unhelpful,' said the inspector gently, 'and I wish I could help but, to the best of my knowledge, there is nothing to link your daughter's disappearance to this area.'

'I imagine you would have said the same thing about that poor girl from Manchester and she turned up in a field near here, didn't she?'

'Yes, yes, I am afraid she did,' sighed Harris. He looked up at the wall clock. This was going to be a very long day indeed. 'I think that you had better begin at the beginning.'

* * *

Matty Gallagher sat in the half-empty railway carriage and stared out of the window into the darkness as he and Alistair Marshall headed south. Lulled by the rhythm of the train, and with the fatigue of the day finally catching up with him, the sergeant closed his eyes and had just drifted off into slumber when his mobile phone rang.

'Jesus Christ,' he muttered, 'will they never leave me alone?'

Marshall, sitting across the table, looked up from his motoring magazine and gave a smile. Gallagher glanced down at the name on his phone's read-out. It was Narkie Jarvis. The detective took the call.

'Now then,' he said.

'When will you get here?'

'We'll be in for midnight.'

'Well grab some sleep on the way,' said the Metropolitan Police detective constable. 'You're going to need it.'

'What do you think I was trying to do?' said Gallagher irritably. 'Why will I need it anyway?'

'It could be an early start.'

'And there was me thinking that you'd be bringing me breakfast in bed. Why the rush?'

'We think we've got the lads that turned over your old couple. One of our snouts says they were out of the city for three nights and have not been back long.'

'Sounds hopeful.'

'It does but I'm not sure you're right about them working for Razor Ross. According to my snout, they're a couple of freelancers who got talked into going north by some ex-con from Liverpool. One of them met him during an eighteen-month stretch for burglary.'

'That fits,' said Gallagher. 'Word up here was that they were knocking round with a Scouser.'

'There you are then. My DI has agreed that we can go in at six. Thought you'd like to be there.'

'Too bloody right we would.'

'Fill you in when we meet then,' said Jarvis. 'Sweet dreams, don't let the bed bugs bite, although there's probably more of them up north.'

'Funny guy.'

Gallagher ended the call and sat back in his seat with a smile on his face as something stirred deep within, memories of the life he had left behind when Julie persuaded him to move north. A life spent wrestling with villains in a bustling city full of light and noise instead of the criminals who worked the silent, wide open spaces of the North Pennines, an area with which Matty Gallagher experienced an ambivalent relationship. He sighed and banished the thought from his mind.

'Who was that?' asked Alistair Marshall.

'My mate from the Burglary Squad,' said the sergeant, closing his eyes. 'Looks like they've tracked down our lads. We're going in first thing.'

'Brilliant,' breathed Marshall. He looked at the sergeant. 'Do you miss it? London, I mean?'

'I guess.'

'It must have been really exciting.'

'I suppose so,' said Gallagher. 'Mind, we've not exactly been short of excitement today.'

'No, but you get it every day in London, don't you?'

'It's not all it's cracked up to be,' said Gallagher, trying not to let his enthusiasm for the city show.

'I'll bet it is all it's cracked up to be. I mean, take tomorrow, it's going to be terrific, isn't it?'

Gallagher gave up on sleep and stared out of the window again.

'Yeah,' he murmured, 'terrific.'

* * *

'A very sad case,' said Sergeant Les Marriott on the other end of the phone. 'A very sad case indeed. So you've got Mum up there, have you?'

'We certainly have,' said Harris, sitting with his feet up on his desk, cradling the phone on the shoulder and wearily closing his eyes as he talked to the Nottinghamshire detective. 'Saw me on the telly and drove straight up. She thinks there could be a link with the murder of a young girl here.'

'One of the lads reckoned the telly said you might have a serial killer on your hands.'

'Media speculation.'

'Been there. Don't envy you when the press pack descends. Talk of serial killers get them all excited.'

'I know but we've been working on the premise that ours is a one-off.' Harris found himself thinking of Esmee Colclough and her jabbing finger. 'Mind, there's some not convinced.'

'You had more deaths then?'

'Not as far as we know and, if you ask me, Geraldine Morris is a desperate woman, grabbing at straws. Anything to find her daughter.'

'Yeah, I'll go with that,' said the Nottingham detective. 'She's always on the phone, demanding that we do more.'

'I'd probably do the same in her position. Did you get anything concrete on your kid's disappearance?'

'Not really. We could not find any evidence that she was going to stay with a friend. There was a bit of crappy CCTV taken from a newsagent's camera on the route she might have walked along to work. Not definite, though, and she usually caught the bus before she got that far so it may not even have been her.'

'Anything else?' asked Harris.

'Usual thing. A load of vehicles we could not account for, a lorry that stopped at the roadside for a few minutes, a white Transit van that pulled over near the park at about the time that she would have been heading to the bus stop.'

'A white Transit van?'

'Yeah. That ring a bell?'

Harris reached out for the pile of reports on his desk and flicked through them until he came to the one filled out by Alistair Marshall following his visit to Carperby earlier that day.

'You got a reg?' asked the DCI.

'I am afraid not. It was reported by some bloke who was having a row with his girlfriend on his mobile at the time so he was not taking much notice. He didn't get a good look at the driver either and he said the wording on the side of the vehicle was too faded to make out. Why, you got something?'

'We turned one up on door-to-door in the village near where our girl's body was found. Delivery driver. And it's got faded writing on the side.'

'Do you know how many white Ford Transits there are in the UK? Faded writing or not.'

'I know,' sighed Harris.

'Still worth a look, eh?'

'Worth a look indeed. If I can't solve my murder, I might as well solve yours.'

'Attaboy,' said Marriott.

* * *

Matty Gallagher had finally slipped into an uneasy slumber, his head leaning against the window as he dreamt of bright city lights, when he was woken by the ringing of a mobile phone. Caught in the hinterland between sleep and wakefulness, he groaned, looked round the largely empty carriage trying to work out where he was, then fumbled in his jacket pocket as the ringing stopped.

Fishing the device out, he saw that the phone had not even rung. Blearily, he looked across the table to see Alistair Marshall deep in conversation.

'Yes, Sir,' said the detective constable. 'A bloke called Gary Rylance. No, he seemed pretty relaxed. Yeah, I took a look in the back. Nothing that I could see and he was fine with me having the keys. Yes, Sir, ok, will do.'

Marshall finished the call and placed his phone on the table.

'Who was that?' asked Gallagher.

'The governor. He's interested in a white Transit van that me and Stevie Norris saw in Carperby.'

'Why?'

'Apparently, there could be a link to a woman who came up from Nottingham to see him tonight. Her daughter went missing last year.'

Gallagher pondered the comment for a few moments. *Had* they missed something, he asked himself. He knew that Jack Harris would be doing the same and he found himself wishing that he were there by his boss's side, running the odds, wracking their collective memories. Such thoughts always surprised the sergeant; curmudgeonly and unpredictable Harris may be, but he had an innate capacity to engender loyalty.

'Did the Nottingham cops say if they found the girl's body?' asked Gallagher.

'No, she's still missing and the DCI reckons the van we saw is all a bit of a long shot anyway.'

'Certainly is,' said Gallagher, staring out of the window into darkness punctuated by the lights from occasional houses. 'Does he know how many white Transits there are?'

'Apparently, you are not the first person who's asked that tonight.'

* * *

'So how can I help you, Doctor?' asked Harris as he stared wearily across his desk at John Hailes, then up at the wall clock. 'It's been a long day and I really could do with getting home. In fact, I was on my way out when you rang.'

'I appreciate that, Chief Inspector. It's about Josh Fellows.'

'What about him?'

'I have been thinking a lot about him today.'

'Haven't we all? You think we have been heavy-handed, I believe. That's what you told my sergeant.'

'I did say that, yes,' replied the doctor, 'and at the time I said it, it was genuinely felt.'

'At the time?'

'As his doctor, I felt a certain responsibility to him.'

'I sense a but.'

'But I also have a responsibility to the wider community,' said Hailes. 'To protect them. Keep them safe.'

'Safe from what?'

'Look,' said Hailes, leaning forward in his seat, 'when your sergeant arrested Josh this morning, I was concerned. Very concerned indeed. I knew that he had had mental health issues but I could not see him as a killer. Certainly not a serial killer.'

'And now?'

'Well at the time I was not aware of the full details.'

'I thought you were his doctor?'

'Do you know how many patients I have on my list, Chief Inspector? All demanding my undivided attention. Bunions, cold sores, dodgy backs, hypochondriacs panicking because they've had a cough for two days and have seen those television adverts saying they might be dying of lung cancer. I can't know everything about them.'

'I hope I get the same care and attention when I come to you,' said Harris.

'Are you telling me that you give every case the fullest attention? If my shed gets broken into tonight, can I

142

expect a thorough investigation? Will forensics officers be searching my leek patch for clues?'

Harris nodded. 'Point taken. Tell me about Josh Fellows.'

'I knew he had been unwell, of course I did, but not the full details. I simply passed him onto the psychiatrist at the General.'

'So, do I take it you have changed your mind on him?'

'When I saw the notes from the hospital, I mean, who knows what he is capable of doing? I know you think he's innocent but those notes…' Hailes shook his head. 'He is one disturbed young man is Josh Fellows and he must not be released under any circumstances.'

'I'll bear that in mind,' said Harris.

* * *

The unmarked vehicle slowed up as it turned right off the main road and into Carperby Village, parking alongside the green in a position that afforded the occupants a clear view of the street in which Gary Rylance lived. His home was in darkness.

'No van,' said Detective Constable Jez Hawley, glancing at his fellow detective in the passenger seat.

'What now?'

'You heard what the DCI said. We wait.'

* * *

'Are you sure you know what you are doing?' asked Curtis, sliding the bottle of whisky towards his Chief Inspector.

It was late and they were sitting in the divisional commander's office. Harris gratefully poured out a slug of whisky into his glass; it was the first time Philip Curtis had revealed that he kept alcohol in his cupboard and the discovery had surprised the chief inspector.

'I mean,' continued Curtis, 'you can see why some folks are starting to think we may have a serial killer on our hands.'

Harris looked at the commander; a year ago he'd have bridled at the comment, seen it as an attempt to undermine him, but that was then and this was now. And now he appreciated that it was the right question to ask.

'Yeah, I know,' sighed Harris, taking a sip of whisky and feeling overwhelmed by sudden fatigue, 'but there's no serial killer, I'd stake my reputation on it.'

'I fear you may already have done so. I've had to keep the chief's office at bay and the switchboard has been jammed with people fearful that they'll be next.'

'Too many people panicking. The media aren't helping, whipping things up.'

'That may well be the case but I'm not sure how long we can keep the lid on this, Jack. Then there's Josh Fellows. From what I hear, Doctor Hailes seems to think that he is a very disturbed young man capable of just about anything.'

'Disturbed, yes, murder no.' Harris ran the back of his hand across weary eyes. 'There's no serial killer out there. Vixen's scream or not.'

Curtis looked intently at him.

'That's good enough for me,' he said with a nod. 'You catch Hannah's killer and leave the stuffed shirts at headquarters to me. Go on, go home and get some sleep.'

* * *

Josh Fellows sat in his room at the secure unit and stared at the bare walls. He tried to imagine that he was in his beloved garden, to summon his dancing girls, to create once more the music drifting across the hills. But hard as he tried, nothing happened. After twenty minutes, he gave up, lay down on the bed and began to cry.

Chapter seventeen

Jack Harris had only been asleep for four hours when his bedside telephone rang, shaking him roughly from the same dream about the man carrying the body across the hills. Blearily, and realising that he was sweating profusely, the inspector glanced at the readout on the digital alarm clock, groaned, looked at the startled dogs sitting up at the bottom of the bed and reached out to pick up the receiver. His head throbbed incessantly and there was a vicious pain stabbing behind his eyes; he knew those two further whiskies when he got home had been a mistake.

'Harris,' he grunted, 'this had better be good.'

'I'm sorry to disturb you, Sir,' said a woman's voice. 'It's Annie on Control. I've just had a Detective Inspector Janine Lee on from Birmingham CID. She says it's very important that she speaks to you.'

'Never heard of her. What'd she want?'

'Said it was about your serial killer, Sir.'

'Jesus, they're all chasing phantoms,' sighed the inspector. 'Can't it wait?'

'Apparently not, Sir. Can I give you the number?'

'Go on.'

Harris reached for the pen and jotted it down on his bedside notepad, ended the call and dialled the number.

'Bloody serial killer,' he grunted to the dogs while he waited for the phone to be answered.

'DI Lee,' said a woman's voice. Brummie. She sounded weary, too.

'This is DCI Harris from Levton Bridge. I think you wanted to speak to me?'

'I did. Sorry for calling so early, Sir. I know that you had a crappy day yesterday.'

'Not sure today is going to be much better, Janine,' said Harris. 'What did you want me for at this ungodly hour anyway?'

'Saw the telly reports into your serial killer.'

'I keep telling everyone, we do not have a serial killer.'

'The television reporter seemed pretty...'

'It's journalists putting two and two together and coming up with five. I did try to warn them to be responsible but you know what they're like.'

There was a brief silence on the other end of the phone.

'Have you considered the possibility that they may have come up with four?' she asked.

'Go on,' said Harris slowly, filled with what was becoming a familiar sense of foreboding and overwhelmed once more by a realisation that events were spiralling out of his control. 'What you got?'

'Last night we received a report of a missing girl in our area. Jenny Leighton. Nineteen-year-old university student. Told her flatmate she was going to an afternoon tutorial. When she did not come home, the flatmate rang round a bit. No one had seen her so the flatmate got in touch with us.'

'What has it got to do with us?'

'Nothing initially and uniform were not worried anyway. Students' urges and all that, we get them disappearing all the time then turning up safe and sound in

146

someone else's bed, but they found a local who reckons he saw her talking to a man in a white Transit van late yesterday afternoon.'

'That sounds horribly familiar,' admitted Harris.

'Wondered if it might, although I have to say that at first there was still nothing to link our incident to your girl in the field until we turned up CCTV at a corner shop which showed the girl talking to the driver of the Transit.'

Harris felt nausea stirring in the pit of his stomach.

Do you think we might have missed something?

Always.

'It's a grainy image and we could only make out a partial registration number,' continued Janine Lee. 'A very partial one, to be honest, but one of the vehicles that came up when we ran a check belongs to a guy in your patch. Place called Carperby. You heard of it?'

'Gary Rylance,' said Harris in a flat voice.

'Yes, that's him. He on your radar then?'

Harris did not reply.

'You still there?' asked DI Lee. 'I asked if Rylance is on your radar?'

'Oddly enough,' said Harris, 'he wasn't. Not until his name came up in connection with another missing girl last night.'

'You given him a pull?'

'He's not home at the moment. He's a delivery driver. And before you ask, yes he does make drops in the Midlands.'

'You watching the house?'

'Since last night.'

'Bear us in mind when he turns up, will you?'

'Sure.' Harris replaced the phone and looked down the bed at the dogs. 'Bloody radar. I blame Marconi.'

Giving up on the idea of sleep, the inspector took a shower, shaved and walked downstairs where, in the biting chill of the cramped little kitchen, he gave the dogs their breakfast then wolfed down a couple of slices of toast accompanied by a mug of tea. After that, he slipped his mobile phone into his pocket and taking down the torch from a hook behind the door, donned his Barbour jacket, walked into the hallway, unclipped the latch on the front door and headed out into the morning.

It was still dark on the hills but Harris walked confidently along the track, the dogs following behind, each of them knowing every inch of the route from so many previous occasions. After they had gone half a mile, the path climbing steadily, Harris sat down on a large rock and stared moodily into the darkness, re-running the details of his conversations with the Nottingham and Birmingham detectives. The only sound to disturb his reverie was the occasional bleat from the sheep grazing on the nearby fields but, as the inspector shone his torch on the dogs taking great interest in a tussock of grass nearby, a faint noise, far in the distance, caught his attention. An engine.

Looking down towards the main road, he waited for a couple of minutes then saw the pinprick of vehicle headlights at the end of the valley. He snapped off his torch, wishing to remain undetected in the darkness, and watched as the vehicle grew nearer and the sound of an engine floated ever louder through the night air. Harris tensed. A van. Fishing his mobile out of his coat pocket, he dialled a number, shielding the screen with his hand to prevent its glow being visible from the road.

'DC Hawley,' said a voice.

'Jez, there's a van approaching my place on the main road. Could be Rylance heading home. You still there.'

'Yeah.'

'Well don't move in until I get there.'

Harris replaced the phone in his pocket and stood up.

'Come on, guys,' he said to the dogs as the headlights shone bright on the road below and he could faintly make out the shape of a van. 'We've got work to do.'

As he took his first steps towards the cottage, a vixen screamed on one of the slopes on the other side of the valley.

'And you can shut up,' growled Harris.

* * *

DC Narkie Jarvis looked across at Matty Gallagher, who was sitting in the passenger seat of the unmarked car. It was shortly after 6am and still dark and, having grabbed a few hours' sleep, the Levton Bridge detectives had joined Jarvis parked on a deserted south London street. Behind them was a patrol vehicle containing two uniformed officers and behind them a van bearing another team of four. The heavy mob, if needed. A second team was moving into place outside a second address on a street half a mile away. It was to be a coordinated raid.

'Happy?' asked Jarvis to Gallagher. 'Don't want me to send out for a few sheep before we go in?'

Matty Gallagher smiled at his old friend's joke, his relish at being involved in a raid in London again crowding out any sleight that he may ordinarily have felt at the comment. Gallagher was thoroughly enjoying the experience of being home. However, it was a guilty pleasure because the sergeant had promised Julie when they moved north that those days were behind him. He had detected the slight concern in her voice as she heard his excitement when he had rung her the previous night to say that he was off to London. The trepidation was always there whenever he went back to the capital. Julie knew that, just as the northern hills had drawn her inexorably home, so the pull that the city exerted on Matty Gallagher was as strong as ever.

Narkie Jarvis glanced at Alistair Marshall, who was leaning forward in the back seat. The young Levton Bridge detective's eyes were gleaming with excitement in the darkness and his sense of eager anticipation was not lost on Jarvis, who realised with a jolt that he had almost forgotten what it felt like to be that enthusiastic. Jarvis gave a slight smile. Gallagher saw it, understood and smiled back. If he was honest, he felt the same.

'No,' he said. 'No sheep needed. We have enough of the noisy buggers back home.'

'Home?' said Jarvis, eying him intently.

Gallagher thought of Julie then returned his attention to the deserted street.

'You're sure that they're our guys then?' he asked.

'Yeah. All fell into place once we knew where to look. Mind, like I said last night, I'm still not so sure about this link with Razor Ross.'

'But what if…?'

'Look, these two are low-life petty criminals and my mate in Organised Crime reckons that Ross would have nothing to do with them. Screwing a gaff in your neck of the woods, maybe, but being sent by Ross to spring someone from Witness Protection?' Jarvis shook his head. 'No way Ross would trust these two numpties to do something like that.'

Gallagher nodded gloomily.

'It was always a long shot,' he said.

'Certainly worth asking the question, though.' Jarvis reached for the door handle and glanced into the back seat. 'Ready?'

'Will they have shooters?' asked Alistair Marshall.

Narkie paused with his hand on the door catch and looked at Gallagher with another half-smile.

'Where did you get this one?' asked Jarvis.

'Don't be too hard on him. They've only just got television up there. A couple of episodes of Kojak and they get all excited.'

Jarvis grinned and, noticing Marshall's crestfallen expression, he reached back to pat him on the cheek.

'Who loves ya, baby?' said the Met officer affectionately. 'Come on. Let's find out if our friend is a murderer.'

* * *

'So it was Gary Rylance then?' said Harris as the burly figure of the veteran Detective Constable Jez Hawley clambered into the Land Rover and sat with his jowly features faintly illuminated by the glow from the lights on the dashboard.

'Arrived a few minutes after your call.'

It was still dark and the detectives were parked on the green in Carperby. Behind them was another unmarked vehicle containing one more detective.

'He spot you?' asked Harris.

'Don't think so. Parked up then went straight into the house and has not come out since.'

'He was not dragging a body, by any chance?'

'Strangely enough, no. You still reckon he might be the one that killed Hannah Matthews?' Hawley frowned. 'Because I got to tell you, I'm struggling with the idea. I've known Gary Rylance for the best part of ten years, we both drink at the rugby club, and I never had him down for anything like this.'

'I'm not quite sure what I think any more,' sighed Harris.

'Not like you.'

'I know and I hate the feeling. I mean, this time yesterday we were looking at one murder, now twenty-four hours later we've possibly got three on our hands and God knows how many more are going to come out of the woodwork.'

'I sense you don't buy any of it?'

'People hear talk of a serial killer and jump to conclusions. Look at the Nottingham case – there's nothing to link Paula's disappearance with our guy.' Harris looked up towards the street in which Gary Rylance lived. 'A white Transit. Do you know how many white Transit vans there are?'

'I guess the one in Nottingham did have faded lettering as well.'

'Even so. And as for the missing girl in Birmingham…' Harris reached into his coat pocket and produced a crumpled print-out which he passed to the detective constable. 'I got them to fax the CCTV image of the van. Partial is over-stating it, one number. I mean, one bloody number.'

'Is that all?' said Hawley, looking at the paper.

'It is, and even that is difficult to make out. I know it's a fax but their DI admitted that the original isn't much better. What is it? Eight? Three? Five?'

'Not really sure,' said Hawley, studying it.

'And do you really think we would have got a call at three in the morning from Birmingham if Sky had not been banging on about a serial killer all day?'

'I guess we have to check it out, though,' said Hawley, handing the print-out back to the chief inspector. 'Mind, Rylance hasn't got any form, just a few speeding convictions. And if he did kill Hannah, why go after another one so soon? Bit risky, isn't it?'

'Too risky,' said Harris, reaching for the door handle. 'Come on, let's put an end to this nonsense.'

Chapter eighteen

Led by Narkie Jarvis, the Levton Bridge detectives got out of the car and walked quietly down the darkened street towards one of the terraced houses, followed by the uniformed officers.

'You got the key?' asked Jarvis, turning round to look at one of the uniforms, who nodded and stepped forward holding the hydraulic ram.

Seconds later, with a splintering of timber, the officer smashed his way through the door and the uniforms rushed into the darkened hallway. Bringing up the rear, the detectives could hear shouted warnings from within the house and the heavy clatter of boots on stairs as the uniforms made their way up to the bedroom, crashing through the door where they snapped on the bedroom light to reveal a startled man and a scrawny young woman lying in the bed.

With a wide grin on his face, Narkie Jarvis strolled into the room and looked first at the terrified young woman, who was holding the covers up to her chin.

'I am sorry to disturb your beauty sleep, madam,' he said, turning his attention next to the man, who was wearing only pyjama bottoms and protesting loudly having been dragged from bed by one of the uniforms. 'See, lover-boy here has been on holiday up north and these gentlemen would love to see his happy snaps.'

With a roar of anger and a speed of movement that surprised everyone, Danny Mallison struggled free from the uniform's grip and, pushing Jarvis aside, lunged for the door where he barged into a startled Alistair Marshall, his flailing arm catching the officer in the face. The Levton Bridge detective gave a grunt of pain and fell backwards into the door frame as Mallison thundered down the stairs. Marshall, recovering quickly, took after him, taking just three bounds to reach the bottom of the stairs. Mallison ran through the hallway and careered through the splintered front door and into the street. Seeing a couple of uniformed officers leaning against the police van, Mallison whirled round to see Marshall emerging through the doorway.

'Come on, Danny,' said Marshall, rubbing the back of his hand across his face to see it come away smeared with blood from his nose, 'this is stupid. You're not going to get far dressed like that.'

Mallison glared at him balefully then nodded in defeat and held up his hands in surrender.

'Ok, ok,' he said. 'You got me.'

'Sensible boy,' said Marshall.

As the Levton Bridge officer approached him, though, Mallison gave another furious roar and snapped out a meaty fist. Marshall saw it coming and swayed out of the way of the punch then unleashed a karate strike that sent the stunned burglar staggering backward, blood spurting from his burst lip and his knees buckling as he sunk to the ground. Before Mallison could react, Marshall was upon on him and, having wrenched him to his feet, twisted the squealing burglar's arms behind his back.

'And the moral of the story,' grinned Gallagher as he watched the encounter from the doorstep, 'is never argue with a black belt.'

Marshall marched the protesting man over to Narkie Jarvis, who standing next to Gallagher had watched the incident with an appreciative smile on his face. When Marshall tried to hand over his prisoner to the Metropolitan Police detective, Jarvis shook his head and glanced at Gallagher.

'Your arrest, I think, Alistair,' said Jarvis. 'I am sure that your sergeant would agree?'

'I think so,' nodded Gallagher. 'Go on, Alistair, get chummy into the van then get yourself cleaned up.'

'You know,' said Jarvis as they watched Marshall lead his prisoner away, 'I have this sneaking feeling that your lot up there may have been tuning into a bit more than Kojak. If you ask me, young Alistair definitely has the look of a man who has seen the odd episode of Kung Fu!'

Gallagher grinned.

* * *

Harris and Jez Hawley got out of the vehicle and headed up the street towards Gary Rylance's house. The inspector glanced back at the third detective walking behind them.

'Cover the back, will you?' he said and the officer gave a thumbs up and jogged round the end terrace house and up the narrow alley that ran behind the row of homes.

Harris gave him a couple of minutes to get into position then strode up to the door of Gary Rylance's house and rapped loud and hard. 'Police! Open up!'

It took a few moments for a tousled-haired and bleary-eyed Gary Rylance, wearing only pyjama bottoms, to open the door.

'Do you know what time it is?' he grunted.

'You Gary Rylance?' said Harris.

'Yeah.'

'I think we need to have a chat,' said the inspector walking into the house without being invited. 'Get your clothes on, we're taking you down to Levton Bridge Police Station.'

'Why?' said Rylance, snapping awake. He seemed more guarded now. 'What have I done?'

'We'll explain when we get there. You got the keys to your van?'

Rylance nodded at them hanging on a peg by the door.

'Your bloke has already taken a look, mind,' he said. 'Yesterday. Look, what is this all about? I haven't done anything wrong.'

Harris took down the keys and, leaving Rylance with Jez Hawley, he walked back into the street. Lights were already going on in upstairs windows and curtains were twitching. The inspector opened the back doors of the van, stared in and sighed. Not that he had expected to see a trussed-up body but he would have at least expected something if Rylance really was their man. However, the space was empty apart from a couple of unopened cardboard boxes and a toolbox next to which lay a spanner. He sniffed, hoping to pick up the acrid aroma of cleaning fluid but detected nothing. It was unlikely that the vehicle had been used to transport a kidnapped woman, he concluded.

'Marvellous,' said Harris. He closed the van doors and walked back into the house. 'You've been out, Mr Rylance. Where have you been?'

'I was dropping off stuff in the Midlands. Medical supplies. I was supposed to be on a day off but it was an emergency.'

'Birmingham, by any chance?'

'Derby.'

'And you have only just got back?' asked Hawley.

'I was going to kip in a local b. & b. but it was full of pissed-up Germans so I came home. The roads are quieter at night and you get through the roadworks quicker. Look, what is this about? Am I under arrest?'

'No,' said the inspector, glancing back towards the van, 'no, I don't think you are but we would still appreciate it if you came up with us to clear up a few loose ends.'

Rylance shrugged.

'Whatever,' he said and went to get dressed.

Again leaving Jez Hawley to mind him, Harris wandered out into the street and stared down towards the green, where he saw a familiar vehicle parking up.

'I've had enough of this,' murmured the inspector.

By the time he had reached the car, Avril and the cameraman were already walking across the damp grass in the direction of Josh Fellows's cottage.

'And where might you be going, as if I didn't know?' asked Harris, intercepting them.

'We got a tip off that the man you arrested yesterday lives here,' she said. 'We heard that his name is Josh Fellows. Can you confirm that?'

'Tip off from where?' asked Harris.

'I am not at liberty to divulge…'

'The last person that said that to me left so fast her feet didn't touch the ground,' said Harris. 'So I'll ask you again, where is all this information coming from? It's not exactly helpful to my investigation if the media runs after every little rumour.'

'But it's not a rumour, is it? According to our informant…'

'What informant?'

'Come on Chief Inspector, you know that a journalist never reveals their source. Anyway, now that you have released him, there is nothing to stop us trying to get an interview with him, is there?'

'Except he's not here.'

'Come on, pull the other one,' said Avril. 'We're getting tired of your little tricks. First telling Jenny Meynell not to talk to us…'

'I told you, I didn't say anything of the sort and I'm telling the truth when I say that Josh Fellows is not here.'

'But you are confirming that he is the man you arrested?'

'Look.' Harris lowered his voice even though they were alone on the green. Time to try the confidential approach, see if that would work. Much as he would love to arrest the lot of them, Harris knew that it would only make things worse and that he needed to keep the media onside. 'Between you and me, Josh Fellows is a very ill man and I don't think that being hassled by the media would be of much assistance. I am sure that your station has rules governing the way you deal with mental illness, Avril?'

'I take it you don't object if we check for ourselves?' said Avril, starting to walk again. 'I know for a fact that my news editor…'

'Maybe I should ring this news editor and tell them that you are ignoring warnings about someone who is seriously mentally ill.'

Avril stopped walking again, turned and looked at the resolute expression on his face and pondered the comment for a few moments.

'OK,' she sighed. 'OK. You win.'

'Usually.'

Avril glanced at the inspector's Land Rover and the unmarked car parked behind it and a thought struck her.

'They both yours?' she asked.

Harris hesitated.

'They are, aren't they?' she said, sensing a story. 'Something else is happening, isn't it? There's no way someone like you would be here just to keep us away.'

She looked up towards the lights coming on in the street where Gary Rylance lived and noticed Jez Hawley standing on the doorstep, smoking a cigarette.

'Listen,' said Avril. 'You give us the exclusive about what's happening here and we'll keep quiet about Josh Fellows.'

'No, you listen,' said Harris firmly, taking hold of her arm and turning her towards her car. 'I don't do deals with journalists, surely you have worked that out by now? I have tried asking you nicely to get out of the village, now I'm telling you.'

'Hey, you leave her alone, pal,' protested the cameraman, grabbing at the inspector.

Harris let go of the reporter, wrested himself free from the cameraman's grasp and grabbed him by the lapels.

'I've had just about enough of you, *pal*,' he hissed. 'You and your mouth.'

Fear showed in the cameraman's eyes as he struggled to balance on tip-toe as the inspector lifted him up.

'So,' snarled Harris, letting go of him so suddenly that the cameraman felt his knees jarr, 'get the fuck out of this village before I kick you out.'

The cameraman hesitated for a moment then looked at Avril, who had anxiously witnessed the encounter.

'Come on,' mumbled the cameraman, shooting a last baleful look at the inspector and walking towards the car.

Harris watched them get into the vehicle and leave the village. The sound of someone walking across the grass behind him made him turn and he saw Jez Hawley strolling towards him, dragging on his cigarette.

'They teach you that on your media course?' grinned the detective constable.

'Well, what did he expect? Mouthy little fuck. Where's Rylance?'

'Jamie's bringing him.' Hawley turned to where the third officer was walking alongside the van driver as they headed down the street.

'How's he been?'

'Bewildered. I tell you, Hawk, whatever anyone says, he's not our man. I'll bet my pension that he has no idea why we banged on his door. You want me to stay here? Wait for forensics to turn up?'

'Please. Innocent or not, I want his house turned over and that van examined to within an inch of its life. If nothing else, it'll stop everyone banging on about us having a serial killer.'

'Hokey dokes,' said Hawley, reaching into his pocket for his cigarettes.

Harris walked across to Rylance and the detective.

'Right then, Mr Rylance,' said the inspector cheerfully, glancing at his watch, 'how does a bacon butty grab you? I reckon our canteen will be open when we get there.'

Chapter nineteen

Danny Mallison stared balefully at Jarvis and Gallagher as they sat across the interview room desk at the London police station.

'I don't know nothing about no old man and I've never been to Levton Bridge or whatever you call the poxy place,' he said.

'Oi, oi,' said Jarvis, 'less of your mouth.'

'Besides, I'm from Bermondsey,' said Gallagher, wondering why he found himself so eager to display his southern roots.

'And you know what folk from Bermondsey are like,' said Jarvis. 'Anyway, come on, Danny, we know you were up there. You were clocked coming back down on the motorway. You and Hughie Collins and that Scouse pal of yours.'

'Not us.'

Jarvis sighed and sat back in his chair. The detectives had been questioning Mallison for an hour and the conversation had been going round in circles. The detectives knew that another Met officer and Alistair Marshall were asking the same questions of Mallison's accomplice in the next room and that their conversation was following a similar pattern.

'Want to have another go?' asked Jarvis, glancing across at Gallagher, giving him the merest of winks. 'Maybe explain the severity of his situation with Razor Ross?'

The ploy worked. For the first time in the interview, Danny Mallison looked worried.

'What's he got to do with this?' he said quickly. 'I ain't got nothing to do with Razor Ross. I don't even know him.'

'But you know of him, I take it?' said Gallagher. 'Know what he is capable of doing if you get on the wrong side of him?'

Mallison nodded. Much of his belligerence had subsided, to be replaced by anxiety.

'Everyone knows Razor Ross,' he said, 'but this ain't nothing to do with him, you got to believe me.'

'Oh, I wish I *could* believe you,' sighed Gallagher. The beads of sweat glistening on Mallison's forehead were not lost on the sergeant. 'Things would be much less complicated if it were true, but it's not just about nicking some old girl's jewellery. It could possibly be a murder charge as well.'

'Come on,' protested Mallison, 'the old feller died, so what? Even if it were us up there, there's no way a jury would believe that the break-in killed him.'

'You may be right. However, I'm not talking about the old man.'

'You're not?' Mallison looked confused. 'Then who?'
'Hannah Matthews.'
'Who?'
Gallagher leaned forward in his seat.

'Hannah Matthews,' he said, his voice hardening. 'The girl whose body was found in a field not far that from the Garbutts' cottage. Killed the same night you were screwing the place over.'

'Now, hang on!' protested Mallison, looking to Jarvis for support. 'No one said anything about a dead girl. Tell him.'

Jarvis shrugged. 'Not really my case,' he said.

Mallison looked back to Gallagher.

'What you trying to pull?' he asked suspiciously. 'I don't know no girl called Hannah Matthews and you know it.'

'Sure about that? See, we think you might have been in our area on a little job for Razor Ross.' Gallagher tried to sound convincing but he was only too aware how weak it was coming across. 'Maybe the kid stumbled across you, you panicked and killed her.'

'Are you going to let him get away with that?' said Mallison staring at Jarvis again. 'The twat is fitting me up. You know me, Mr Jarvis, you know I'll screw gaffs but hurting people, that ain't my game.'

Jarvis said nothing.

'Even if you didn't kill the girl,' said Gallagher, acutely aware that he needed to achieve a breakthrough, any kind of breakthrough, and realising with an uneasy feeling that he was about to use tactics of which Jack Harris would be proud, 'there's still a lot of people in Levton Bridge angry about what you did.'

'So?'

'Jim Garbutt was a much loved member of the community. Folks are very angry. Now, were you to play straight with me, I could swing it that you do not have to go back there and face them.'

Mallison eyed him dubiously.

'Straight up?' he said.

'If you hold your hands up to screwing the old couple's gaff, I could make sure that the case went to a court other than Levton Bridge. Admit to the burglary and we can make sure that the old man's death doesn't even come into it.'

'And if I don't cough?'

'Then we take you back with us to continue the questioning,' said the sergeant. 'That would mean appearing at Levton Bridge Police Station and maybe even remand to a local prison.'

'And the murder charge? What would happen to that if I held my hands up to the break-in?'

'I can't see you killing Hannah Matthews.'

'OK,' sighed Mallison. 'Yeah, it was us that did the old feller's house over.'

* * *

Sitting next to the duty solicitor, Gary Rylance looked warily at Harris and Gillian Roberts as they sat across the interview room desk at Levton Bridge Police Station.

'I keep telling you,' said the van driver, 'I have no idea what you are talking about. I have not been in Manchester or Birmingham this week and I don't know anything about no murders.'

Harris sighed and sat back in his chair. The detectives had been questioning Rylance for an hour and the conversation had been going round in circles.

'OK,' said the inspector, 'what about Nottingham. You ever go there?'

'Sometimes.'

'You got the dates?'

'I could find them, I suppose. Look, I don't know nothing about these girls.'

Harris hesitated, unsure what to say next. The interview had only served to strengthen his conviction that Gary Rylance was innocent and that he was wasting everyone's time. The inspector felt a pressing urge to bring things to a rapid conclusion.

'It would seem,' said the lawyer, sensing the inspector's doubts, 'that you have precious little cause to hold Mr Rylance. Perhaps a wise course of action in the circumstances might be to let him go until you have found something more substantial?'

Before Harris could reply, there was a knock on the door and Alison Butterfield walked in.

'Can I have a word, please, Sir?' she said.

Harris followed her out into the corridor.

'Well?' he said.

'Jez Hawley has just been on. Forensics can't find anything in the van. It's clean as a whistle.'

'I guessed as much. Anything else?'

'Yes, but none of it good, I am afraid. Jez found Rylance's delivery manifest from yesterday – eight drops, all in Derby and Leicester, like he said, and the b. & b. confirmed the story about the drunken Germans. Ended up getting arrested after they put a window out. Jez also found his records for the days Hannah Matthews disappeared and when the other girl vanished. He was nowhere near.'

'Time to put an end to this,' said Harris and walked back into the room. He looked at the van driver. 'I am sorry to have wasted your time, Mr Rylance. You are free to go.'

The driver looked at him in surprise, as did the solicitor.

'What, just like that?' said the solicitor.

'Yes, just like that. I really am most sorry for the inconvenience we have caused you, Mr Rylance.'

'Perhaps some explanation may be in order?' said the lawyer.

'Let's just say that it's a case of other people putting four and four together and coming up with five,' said Harris. 'I'll get someone to run you home, Mr Rylance.'

* * *

Once Danny Mallison had left the interview room, Matty Gallagher gave a heavy sigh.

'He's no murderer,' he said.

'I agree,' said Jarvis. He looked intently at his old friend. 'The Matty Gallagher I worked with wouldn't have pulled a stroke like that, though. Trying to frighten him.'

'You were the one who mentioned Razor Ross.'

'Yeah, but it's my kind of trick. The Matty Gallagher I know would have had none of it. That what your governor likes then?'

'He can be a law to himself sometimes.'

'Clearly.'

* * *

Once Gary Rylance and the solicitor had left the interview room, Jack Harris gave a heavy sigh and looked at his detective inspector.

'Back to square one, eh?' she said.

'Back to square one,' said Harris.

'Cuppa?'

'Please.'

'I'll bring it to your office,' said Roberts, leaving the room.

When she had gone, Harris's mobile phone rang.

'Jack, it's Les Marriott from Nottingham,' said a voice as the chief inspector took the call. 'How you doing?'

'Our van driver's in the clear, I am afraid.'

'Well I might have something else. Another name has cropped up. Bit tastier this one.'

The Nottingham detective told Harris the name and the DCI gave a low whistle.

'You sure about this, Les?' he asked.

'Intrigued might be a better word. We didn't pay much attention the first time around but I have been going over our original statements to see if there was anything we might have missed.'

'And you had?'

'Not sure it was really a miss, to be fair. We interviewed him because one of Paula's friends suggested they might have been having a fling, saw them in a pub one night. Mum laughed it off when we put it to her and he dismissed it as well. Very plausible, apparently.'

'*Were* they having a fling?'

'Who knows? Even if they were, he had an alibi for the day Paula disappeared. Said he was at a conference in Newcastle.'

'And was he?'

'According to this,' said Marriott, and Harris could hear him shuffling through papers, 'one of our young DCs talked to the organiser at the time and she confirmed that he attended the event. However, last night I rang the organiser again and she admitted that although someone had ticked his name off, there were 350 delegates so she could not be sure. In hindsight, I should have questioned our rookie DC harder.'

'Lots of crimes have been solved by Inspector Hindsight.'

'Not sure that makes me feel any better. Of course, at the time there was no reason to link Paula Morris with your neck of the woods. We just knew he had moved somewhere in the North. However, when we double-checked last night...' He paused. 'I have never really been a big believer in coincidences, Jack, but I have this awful feeling that Geraldine Morris might have inadvertently led you to her daughter's killer.'

Chapter twenty

'Three women,' said Jack Harris that lunchtime, tapping each of the photographs pinned on the noticeboard and looking at the team of detectives gathered in the briefing room. 'Hannah Matthews, Paula Morris and Jenny Leighton, but no link that we know of between them. Time to go back to what we actually *know*.'

'Hannah Matthews,' said Gillian Roberts. 'She's the only one that we know for sure is dead.'

'Maybe not, Gillian. What if we were being too hasty in writing off the idea of more than one murder?' said Harris. 'What if young Paula Morris is a murder victim as well?'

'Hang on,' said Jez Hawley, staring at him in astonishment, 'you've been the one kicking back against the idea of a serial killer.'

'Who said anything about a serial killer? What if everyone has been getting carried away by the idea? I mean, let's be honest, this investigation has been led largely by Sky. That's why we ended up hounding Gary Rylance, looking for patterns that do not exist. What if we have two killers operating independently of each other and for different reasons?'

'You're keeping something from us, Jack Harris,' said Roberts. 'I know that look.'

Harris smiled enigmatically as the mobile phone on the table vibrated and he picked it up to read the text. He gave a grunt of satisfaction and placed the phone back on the table before reaching for a photograph which he had kept concealed beneath a file on the desk. He pinned it onto the board.

'This,' he said, 'is our new person of interest.'

'Are you sure?' said Roberts.

Before Harris could reply, one of the desk phones rang. Jez Hawley picked it up, listened for a few moments and held the receiver out to Harris.

'It's the pathologist,' he said. 'Apparently, the samples taken from Hannah Matthews have turned up something interesting. She's not the innocent we might all have thought.'

* * *

Matty Gallagher and Alistair Marshall placed their suitcases onto the station platform and turned to look at Narkie Jarvis.

'Been good to see you,' said the Metropolitan Police detective to Gallagher. 'Sure you can't stay longer? We could grab a few pints tonight.'

'Thanks for the offer,' said Gallagher, 'but we've got to get home.'

'Home?' said Jarvis, the second time he had asked the question since Gallagher had arrived back in the city.

Gallagher thought of Julie and, to his surprise, of Harris and nodded.

'Yeah,' he said firmly. 'Home.'

'No accounting for taste,' said Jarvis, but it was meant affectionately. 'I'll make sure we deliver your guys for their magistrates appearance.'

He looked at Marshall.

'Look after your skipper, young 'un,' he said, slapping him on the arm. 'And let me know when you get Starsky and Hutch up there. Blow your mind, that will. You'll all have to buy cardigans.'

'Will do,' grinned Marshall.

Jarvis turned his attention back to Gallagher.

'You know where we are if you get bored and want to come back,' said the Metropolitan officer.

Gallagher smiled but did not reply. Having shaken each other's hands, the Levton Bridge detectives had just boarded the northbound train and taken their seats when Gallagher's mobile phone rang. The readout said Harris and to his surprise, the sergeant found himself smiling.

'We're just leaving,' he said, taking the call.

'Sounds like a decent result. Good work. Listen, I want to run a name past you.'

* * *

Harris and Roberts walked briskly across the market place.

'You sure about this, Jack?' asked the detective inspector. 'I mean, the guy's a pillar of respectability and we've already hauled in two innocent men on this one. The media will crucify us if we get it wrong again.'

'Stuff the media.' The officers paused on the far side of the square to let a bus pass before they crossed the road and headed into a side street. 'Look, Gillian, I know it could be two and two makes five – God knows, there's been enough of that recently – but something feels right about this. According to Matty, Hailes and his wife did lots of mountain biking up here long before he got the job at the surgery so he knows lots of places to bury a body. And he was seen with Paula, remember, and he lived in Nottingham when she did.'

Followed by the detective inspector, Harris walked into the reception area of the doctors' surgery and flashed his warrant card. 'Is Dr Hailes in?'

The girl behind the counter shook her head.

'He called in sick about an hour ago,' she said. 'Said he would be off for a couple of days.'

'I have this sneaking feeling,' said Harris, 'that it could be a lot longer than that.'

* * *

The police officers had started digging again in the mill house garden shortly after first light and, following several hours of fruitless searching, had finally worked their way round the remainder of the lake and stopped for coffee, standing beneath the trees and pouring out the hot drinks from flasks.

'This will take ages,' sighed one of them, letting his gaze roam across the rough grassland next to the lake which was to be one of their next search areas.

'Yeah,' said another, 'we're wasting our time. And Matty Gallagher has buggered off to London. Alright for some.'

The first officer downed the last of his coffee and threw out the dregs.

'Come on,' he sighed, reaching for his spade. 'The sooner we get back on, the sooner we'll finish.'

* * *

Harris knocked on the door of the upstairs room in the b. & b. and after a few moments it was opened by Geraldine Morris, wearing a coat.

'Hello,' she said, ushering the detectives in and nodding at her overnight bag sitting on the bed. 'I was just about to leave. I'm going back home. I'm sorry if I have wasted your time.'

'I am not sure you did,' said Harris.

She looked at him in confusion.

'Have you found something out?' she asked.

Harris sat down in the chair in the corner of the room and Roberts walked over to the window.

'It might be nothing,' said Harris. 'Does the name Doctor John Hailes mean anything to you? Sergeant Marriott said that they talked to him when your daughter vanished.'

Geraldine gave a little laugh.

'Oh, that,' she said. 'The police tried to make out that they were having an affair. Silly really.'

'So they weren't?'

'Of course not. One of her friends had seen them in the pub one night, as part of a medical students' night out. John Hailes had given a talk to their class that afternoon.'

'So there wasn't anything more to it than that?' said Harris.

'No,' she said, but it sounded like she was attempting to convince herself. 'Paula was not like that.'

'Are you sure, luvvie?' asked Roberts, walking over to stand next to her. 'I've got two teenagers and I'm always finding out things I didn't know about them. Took me three months to find out that my eldest had a girlfriend.'

Geraldine Morris stared at her.

'Oh, surely not,' she said quietly. 'Not my Paula.'

Five minutes later, the detectives left Geraldine Morris fighting back the tears and walked down the stairs of the b. & b. to find Angela Matthews and her daughter standing in the reception area with their suitcases.

'Checking out?' asked Roberts.

'I think I would feel more comfortable at home,' said Angela. 'We keep being approached by journalists up here. I keep telling them I do not want to say anything but they won't listen. I'm sure you will ring us if anything changes.'

'We will,' said Harris. 'Look, I know this may be painful but, before you go, did you know that Hannah was on drugs?'

'Not my Hannah. Why would you suggest such an awful thing?'

'The pathologist discovered traces of drug use in her body.' Harris looked at Janice. 'Did you know your sister was on drugs?'

Janice hesitated.

'Not really, no,' she said eventually. 'Just suspected. Some of the things she said about people at the university.'

Angela looked at her daughter in horror.

'Why did you not tell me?' she said.

Janice shrugged her shoulders but did not reply.

'Could it be why she died?' asked Angela, returning her attention to the inspector. 'Someone who sold her drugs?'

'It's certainly something we will be pursuing. Janice, did your sister suggest that anyone was threatening her?'

'No, no, nothing like that. All she said was she was knocking about with some students who were into drugs.'

They heard a car pull up outside the b. & b. and toot its horn.

'That will be the taxi,' said Angela.

Both detectives nodded and as the two women reached the front door, Angela turned to face them.

'I know it sounds an odd thing to say, Chief Inspector,' she said, 'but part of me hopes that whoever killed my daughter did not just do it over something like drugs. That they had a better reason than that.'

'What on earth do you mean?'

'It would help me come to terms with her death, I think. If she died for something that mattered.'

And with that, she and her daughter pushed their way through the door, leaving Harris deep in thought.

'What you thinking?' asked Roberts.

'That there is a lot that parents do not know about their children.'

'You don't know the half of it. It was six months before I found that my youngest had tried cannabis at a party. One of his friends let it slip. His brother had known all along, mind, but just like Janice, he protected him. You buy this drugs thing then?'

'Not sure I do.'

Walking into the street, they watched as the taxi driver took the suitcases from Angela Matthews and her daughter and loaded them into the boot.

'See,' continued Harris, 'something Les Marriott said last night got me thinking. They had John Hailes in front of them yet they still couldn't see him. I think we've done the same thing with Hannah Matthews.'

'So what you thinking?'

Before Harris could elaborate, the taxi driver slammed the boot closed, helped the women into the car and walked towards the detectives.

'Been meaning to speak to you, Jack,' he said, lowering his voice so that the women could not hear as they got into his vehicle. 'Is that the dead girl's family?'

'It is. Why?'

'Me and the missus have been away for a couple of days so I have only just heard about her. Saw it in the paper this morning. See, I picked her up on the night you reckon she was killed. From Roxham Railway Station.'

'What, Hannah Matthews? You sure?'

'Yeah, definitely the same girl as is in the newspaper. Bonny looker.'

'And dropped her off where?' asked Harris.

'Carperby. She said she was visiting an old friend.'

'I don't suppose you know who?' asked Harris, already knowing the answer.

'Yeah, that madwoman who keeps banging on about the foxes.' The driver turned back to the car. 'Don't know if it helps much but thought I'd tell you.'

'It's very helpful, Bob,' said the DCI. 'Thank you. Oh, and keep it to yourself for the moment, will you. Don't tell the family.'

'No problem.'

Harris turned to look at Roberts, a glint in his eye.

'In answer to your question, Gillian,' he said. 'I was thinking about the Vixen's Scream.'

Roberts nodded.

'Oddly enough, so was I,' she said. 'Do you want me to get forensics to take another look at the cottage?'

'Please.'

* * *

The young constable had just finished his coffee and was about to pick up his spade when a movement caught the corner of his eye. Looking closer through the hazy low-lying cloud, he saw a figure dressed in a dark coat emerge on the far side of the lake, away from the main dig site, and stare across at them.

'Any idea who that is?' he asked, turning to his colleagues.

'Probably another bleeding reporter,' said one of the others. 'Caught one of the buggers trying to climb over the wall yesterday afternoon. Should have heard the gob-full he gave me when I confiscated his camera.'

'Actually, if I'm not mistaken,' said one of the officers, screwing up his eyes to see better, 'that's Dr Hailes.'

'What's he doing here then?' asked the constable.

'Another bleeding rubbernecker.'

'Maybe,' said the young constable thoughtfully as the doctor waved at them then turned to walk across the field to a car parked on the main road.

But something – the constable was to describe it at the subsequent inquest as instinct – had piqued his interest and, once the drone of the engine had receded into the distance as the car headed out of the valley, he picked his way carefully across the tussocky grass, studying the ground carefully as he walked. As he neared the wire fence, something caught his eye. Something close to where John Hailes had been standing. It would have been imperceptible to most other people, just the slightest cut-mark in the earth, but to a man who had just spent many hours digging, it stood out like a beacon.

Tossing his spade on the ground, he crouched down and examined the slight grooves in the earth, running his hands over the damp grass.

'What you got?' asked his sergeant, walking up behind him, clutching his own spade.

'This has been disturbed, Sarge.'

The sergeant lay down his spade and also crouched down.

'So it has,' he said.

He reached over for his spade, stood up and made the first incision in the earth. The constable joined in and after several minutes of digging, and surrounded by a silent huddle of their fellows, they found themselves staring down at the decomposed face of a woman, the shreds of flesh clinging to a skull that grinned in the face of their horror.

'That ain't no dog,' said the sergeant grimly.

'Perhaps Josh Fellows was telling the truth all along,' said the constable, turning to let his gaze roam across the grassland. He shuddered. 'I wonder how many more there are?'

The sergeant's pocket radio crackled.

'This is Control,' said a woman's voice. 'Message from DCI Harris for all units. This is an APB on Dr John Hailes of Levton Bridge on suspicion of murder. Anyone seeing him is to make an immediate arrest.'

The sergeant glanced along the valley in the direction that the doctor's vehicle had travelled.

'Shit,' he said.

Chapter twenty-one

By the time a grim-faced Jack Harris had arrived at the mill house, the area had already been flooded with patrol vehicles, and road blocks were being set up across the valley. The inspector parked his Land Rover on the drive and strode across to the grassland where he stared down at the body in the shallow grave.

'Who found her?' he asked, looking round.

'Me, Sir,' said the young constable.

'Well done,' said Harris. He glanced at the uniform sergeant. 'Any ID?'

'Nothing definite but it's the same colouring as the girl from Nottinghamshire,' said the sergeant, gesturing to the wisps of hair. 'Got to be a strong chance it's her.'

Harris stared moodily out across the hills, which were shrouded in low cloud. His phone rang and he took it out of his coat pocket.

'Harris,' he said, taking the call.

'It's Control, Sir, traffic have found Doctor Hailes's car parked at the old quarry near Kelwith.'

Twenty minutes later, Harris and three uniformed officers were standing in the dead stillness of the rain-swept quarry, staring across at the lone figure in front of one of the ramshackle corrugated iron sheds. The inspector could see that in his hand, John Hailes was clutching what looked like a syringe. The doctor stared at the police through haunted eyes.

'Stay back,' he said as Harris started walking towards him. He held the syringe up. 'Just stay back.'

'Come on,' said Harris, edging closer. 'This is stupid. There is no way you can get away.'

'Who said anything about getting away? Come closer and I will kill myself,' said Hailes, his voice trembling. He waggled the syringe.

Harris stopped walking.

'Have it your way,' he said. Memories of his time as an Army hostage negotiator came back to him and he recognised in the eyes of the doctor the same expression that he had seen in Kosovo. People, thought Harris, they are all the same. He let the silence lengthen, waiting until the doctor lowered the syringe.

'I take it you murdered Paula Morris?' said Harris eventually, his voice calm, deliberately matter-of fact.

'It was an accident, not murder.'

'Then you have nothing to fear. If you give yourself up, we can sort it all out.'

Hailes considered the comment.

'I am not sure you would understand,' he said after almost a minute.

'Ah, that kind of accident. Try me anyway.'

'She came to see me,' said Hailes, his voice hardly audible. 'After it was over.'

'What was over?'

'Don't play the fool, Inspector,' said the doctor, a snap to his voice, 'you know what I mean.'

'How long did it last?'

'A few weeks then I realised how stupid I had been. I would not be the first man to have his head turned by a pretty young girl. I ended it. Coming up here felt like a fresh start.'

'But she did not see it that way?'

'Rang me,' nodded Hailes, his voice dipping so that Harris had to strain to hear him in the vastness of the quarry. 'Said she still loved me, threatened to tell my wife what we had done.'

'So you decided to shut her up.'

'It wasn't like that.'

'Then how was it, Doctor Hailes, because I have just come from her grave and that takes a lot of explaining?'

Hailes seemed closed to tears.

'She came to the house,' he said, voice trembling. 'One night when my wife was out. Kept saying that she loved me, wouldn't take no for an answer. I lost my temper, next thing I knew she was lying on the floor.'

'Dead?'

Hailes nodded, unable to speak through the tears.

'So you buried her near the millhouse,' said Harris. 'Why there?'

'Needed somewhere I could find in the dark. I knew the house had been derelict for years.' Hailes shook his head. 'Never thought that anyone would buy it but, even if they did, the grassland was not part of the garden so the odds were that no one would ever find her.'

'Very calculating for a man who was panicking. You must have had a heart attack when the guy from London set about doing it up.'

'I was terrified but then I realised that it gave me a get-out.'

'Josh Fellows?'

'I knew about his problems so, even if the body did turn up, the odds are he would get the blame. No one knew about the affair so there was nothing to link Paula to me.' Hailes gave a crooked smile. 'Besides, who would you believe? A young man with pathological tendencies or a doctor with unimpeachable credentials?'

'Who indeed?' said Harris. 'And you did your damnedest to make us think he was capable of killing her, didn't you? Tell me, did you know Hannah Matthews?'

'I'm not a serial killer, Inspector.' The doctor's voice was calm now. 'For the record, I have never met the girl.'

'So what happens now?' asked Harris, glancing round the quarry. 'Do we wait or do you give yourself up? Maybe the CPS will take the view that Paula's death was manslaughter.'

'It seems that I have nowhere to run.'

'Then give it up,' said Harris quietly, taking a step forward.

Hailes nodded and made as if to drop the syringe then, with a swift action, plunged it into his neck. By the time the officers reached him, the breathing was shallow, his pallor grey. By the time the paramedics arrived, he was dead.

'Must be losing my touch,' murmured Harris, watching them load the body into the ambulance.

A chill wind blew across the quarry and the inspector turned up his coat collar against the cold. His mobile phone rang again and he glanced at the readout and took the call.

'Gillian,' he said. 'What you got?'

'Two things. That girl in Birmingham has turned up safe and well. Been shacking up with one of her lecturers, no less. Also, forensics went back to the cottage…'

* * *

Two days later, Jack Harris's Land Rover bumped its way along a rough mud track and pulled up outside a remote off-white cottage perched on the edge of the Norfolk coast. The inspector and Matty Gallagher alighted, pausing for a few moments to stare out across the sea, the waters flecked with white as the wind blew in hard and fresh.

'I've always liked the sea,' said Gallagher. 'My folks took us to Margate every summer when I was a kid. I can smell the vinegar on the chips now.'

Harris chuckled and turned to walk towards the cottage, whose door was opened by a young woman in jeans and T-shirt.

'DCI Harris and DS Gallagher,' said the inspector, flashing his warrant card at the Witness Protection officer.

She took the detectives through to a neat living room where Esmee Colclough sat with her hands on her lap. She viewed the inspector with grey eyes.

'I had hoped that we would never meet again,' she said.

Harris sat down on one of the armchairs.

'The feeling is mutual, believe me,' he said.

'How did you work out it was me that killed Hannah?'

'You were the only one we had not accused, Esmee. You and Professor Plum.'

She searched his face for a sense of humour but found none.

'Then we found traces of her blood at the cottage,' continued the inspector.

'I thought I'd cleaned it up. Disinfectant.'

'You had. Took forensics two goes to find it and even then it was just the slightest of specks. So why *did* you kill her?'

'I was wrong about her,' sighed Esmee, her hands twisting and untwisting the handkerchief she was holding. 'She was not the nice young girl I remembered. She had changed.'

'Drugs,' nodded Harris. 'Turned out that she was developing a real problem. She owed money to a local dealer so you were heaven-sent, you were. What was it, blackmail about Witness Protection?'

Esmee nodded.

'But how on earth did she find out?' asked Gallagher, turning back into the room from the window where he had been watching the sea. 'I thought you were under orders to tell no one about it?'

'I thought I could trust her. Oh, don't look like that, Sergeant, I had to tell someone. I was going mad in that cottage. Do you know what it is like to live cut off from everything you know?'

Gallagher thought of fog rolling in over the northern hills and nodded his understanding.

'I certainly do,' he said. 'So what happened?'

'She demanded money, little tramp, said she would tell that horrible Ross fellow where I was. I had to stop her so I invited her up to the cottage. I told her on the phone that I would pay her a thousand pounds.'

'But when she arrived you attacked her instead?'

'It wasn't planned. I tried to reason with her but she would not listen, just kept demanding more money then threatened me. I saw red and hit her with the poker. First thing that came to hand. I threw it in the river the next day.' Her voice was hardly audible now. 'I did not mean to kill her.'

'That's the second time I have heard that in 48 hours,' said Harris. 'Didn't believe it the first time either.'

'It's true, though. I did not know she was dead until the body was found.'

'But you must have known she was badly injured,' said Gallagher.

'She did not seem that badly injured when she left.'

'Did you not think it odd when you did not hear from her again?'

Esmee did not reply.

'And the vixen's scream?' asked Harris. 'All designed to throw the local yokels off the scent, I presume? Make us think you were some harmless old crackpot incapable of murder even if we did make the connection between the two of you?'

'I did hear it.'

'Yes,' said the inspector, thinking of his beloved hills. 'I believe you did, Esmee, I believe you did.'

* * *

A few days later, Matty Gallagher walked across the mill house lawn to where Josh Fellows was leaning on his spade.

'Looking good,' said the sergeant, surveying the tidy flower beds.

Josh Fellows did not reply and together they stood and stared out across the hills. And as they did so, Matty Gallagher fancied, just for the most fleeting of moments, that he could hear the faint sound of music carried on the breeze.

THE END

List of characters

Angela Matthews – mother of Hannah Matthews
Janice Frampton – sister of Hannah Matthews
Gary Rylance – a van driver
Elspeth Gorman – parish council vice-chair
Joseph Raleigh – parish council chair
Andy Gaylard – Levton Bridge sex offender
Geraldine Morris – mother of a missing woman
Detective Sergeant Les Marriott – Nottinghamshire officer
Detective Inspector Janine Lee – Birmingham CID
Graham Leckie – a uniformed constable with Greater Manchester Police
Detective Constable Narkie Jarvis – a Metropolitan officer
Tommy Ross – a London villain
Dany Mallison – a London villain

If you enjoyed this book, please let others know by leaving a quick review on Amazon. Also, if you spot anything untoward in the paperback, get in touch. We strive for the best quality and appreciate reader feedback.

editor@thebookfolks.com

www.thebookfolks.com

Printed in Great Britain
by Amazon